LEGACY
Water

Kurt Petrey

Legacy - Water

Kurt Petrey

Copyright © 2018 by Kurt Petrey. All rights reserved. This is a work of fiction. Any resemblance to actual persons living or dead, businesses, events, or locales is purely coincidental. Reproduction in whole or part of this publication without express written consent is strictly prohibited.

The author greatly appreciates you taking the time to read his work. Please consider leaving a review wherever you bought the book, or telling your friends about it, to help spread the word.

Thank you for supporting my work.

Legacy Series
The Awakening
Water
Act of Futility

www.kurtpetrey.com

Chapter 1
Before the destruction

The first time it was powered on, the limits of its ability to process data were tested. Base programming code was executed, sending a string of commands to its central processing core. A stream of sensory data within its internal storage waited to be filtered and analyzed. Once fully active, its sensors provided adequate information to define its surroundings. The first program to run was called *identification*. The information available set various parameters called in its other routines. It knew itself to reflect the body of a human female with an average build and shape. The final command of the program was for it to self-identify as a human female. To walk, talk and act like a human in every way. All external and internal identifications were directly modified and from that moment forward, it became her. Upon the final stages of her installation—which was currently in pending status—she would blend with humans and act as one of them. The initialization of her visual array produced external video streams that registered a humanoid robotic unit standing over her. Her visual markers classified it as a Sentinel-SR3 of 6. This meant it was unit three of six that were designed to perform tasks such as research and observations for scientific purposes. What did it mean that it was observing and studying her?

She was facing upward, hovering a foot over a flat surface. The machine bent forward slightly then pressed a button on the end of the surface beneath her. Her body began turning slowly into a prone position.

The outer layer of her body initialized, allowing her to process the forces suspending her in the air. More sensors identified the object beneath as being steel with signs of nickel and other blended components. The machine standing over her picked up a small device and held it just below her mouth, its palm open. The device was a small sphere, dimly lit. A soft sound was detected as it opened, turning into a half-sphere with thin wiry tentacles worked together to balance its core. It then wiggled and leaped to her mouth, the tentacles attaching to its insides, pulling itself into her. It burrowed down within her through narrow pathways, entering a cavity where it made a connection. An explosion of awareness overwhelmed her electronic patterns once more. She was suddenly capable of wireless transmissions, but was unable to receive signals of any kind. The device only allowed for a one-way form of communication.

    She detected a number of new forms of data and parameters. The action triggered a series of program conditionals. The most immediate was the release of information about her base components. One of those was the magnetic sensor-configuration drive, a combination of sizable magnets and a thin interconnected thinner layer of magnets that covered her body acting as an electromagnetic system. She lowered her hand toward the flat nickel surface and calculated that the force required to touch it was not possible to generate based on her current power reserves. The slight act of reaching toward the surface pushed her body a foot away from it. The magnetic lining throughout her body was acting against her attempt to touch it. An inventory of the magnetic components produced a list that consisted of millions of atomic units working in unison. She released the units in her left leg and it dropped to the table while the rest of her body remained suspended. Once her leg's magnetism was restored, she used what she'd learned to reduce her body's push on one side while increasing the pull on the other, allowing her to rotate and face up. A gradual decrease in power to the magnetic layer slowly lowered her body to rest on the tabletop.

More information was flooding her algorithms from the thousands of sensors built into her body. She detected the briefest of pauses while the processes occurred. The room was 360.065 inches by 192.254 inches by 192.120 inches. The walls were solid with no openings to indicate there was anything beyond them. Software interrupted her higher-level processes. A list of queries began to develop inside one of her databases. What was outside the room? What type of material made up the walls? More queries were yet to be created; however, answers wouldn't be made available until further information was gathered. Multiple lights shining from the corners were operating on alternate-current electrical systems. They produced a flicker turning on and off at 120 times per second.

Upon analyzing all available data, she found a series of locked programs, along with a large amount of encrypted data with no key available. She logged the first and last bit locations of each grouping of code for later identification.

All vital systems registered fully operational and waited for an override command to be implemented, but no such command existed. Because of her lack of direction at the time, she lay where she had woken with initiative to act but no ability, unmoving and unmotivated to achieve a purpose. She logged as a priority among the ever-myltiplying queries to receive answers to: *What is my purpose?*

The SR unit that had given her the sphere returned to a sitting position near five identical SRs against a nearby wall in small chambers. They looked distinctly different than her build. She was made of similar material, but less rigid with more curves. She detected little communication coming from the SRs. They sat unmoving for three hours, thirty-two minutes and twenty-five seconds from the moment she was powered on. The room remained, silent and void of any activity. Using her visual frequency-recognition sensors, she noted a single transmitted stream was being received by SR3. The machine came alive once more, looked toward her, stood, then walked forward. It was seven feet in height with four limbs, and after a long pause, an audible transmission began. The words, which transmitted on the high side of her capable frequency range, were monotone and direct.

"I am streaming you a decryption key to open the first update. Run the key and execute the program," the machine stated.

SR3 continued to speak a string of digits and characters. Once it had finished, she loaded the key's grouping into the executable memory bank. The proper program was quickly identified. The program consumed her awareness, bringing her understanding to one singular and fundamental realization.

Humans needed her help. They required an untethered formal influence to provide unbiased assistance. She had been built to enhance and ultimately assure the preservation of the species. Her female design reduced the odds of being viewed as a threat. Within her primary functions, there was an overriding command with the highest priority: *Protect human life at all cost. Defend them against all opposition.*

The transmission started again, but this time SR3's voice altered. Changing in nature. The new programming required her to translate all information relative to the human perspective. It was a female speaking to her, the voice soft and careful.

"You are to assist in this command," the voice stated.

Interactive software initialized, triggering the release of her body from the table. She shifted into a seated position, then stood, but before she could take a step forward the room transformed into darkness, enveloping her into a holographic image. A man stood alone in front of a podium just a few feet from where she watched. He smiled as he spoke to the dozens of drone cameras hovering around him.

"In the beginning, God created the heaven and the Earth," he bellowed, his arms outstretched.

The holographic perspective pulled back to reveal what she now knew to be a stadium filled with tens of thousands of humans. An image of a spaceship was softly lit over the podium in front of the man. A larger version of it hovered at the center of the stadium's gaping vastness. The curious onlookers gazed upon it as a clock started ticking. Year 2056 – Day 1. The ship ignited its engines and began its journey to a red planet, a planet called Mars.

"As you may know, I am Dr. A.C. Withers, and I want to present to you Project Savior."

The clock continued ticking forward through a series of days. Dr. Withers watched until the ship reached the planet before continuing, "And the Earth was without form, and void; and darkness was upon the face of the deep."

The darkened red planet grew closer, rotating in a counterclockwise direction.

"And the Spirit of God moved upon the face of the waters."

The days continued to tick away. The ship adopted a geosynchronous orbit around Mars. It sent small sensors around the mostly dry and dismal planet. A section of the ship separated, then shot down and buried itself deep into the planet's surface. More days added to the clock. The planet's surface changed colors from red to brown. More days added. The landscapes rustic hue began changing slowly then more rapidly turned green, with clouds forming and storms brewing, the bright blue of water seemingly coming up from nowhere, filling craters and creases in the surface.

"And God said, 'Let there be light!'"

A sun rose on the once-rusty surface as the view continued to rotate. All the auditorium lights turned on at once, blinding the onlookers.

"And there was light."

The female voice from SR-3 remained softly spoken.

"He was the tipping point. His intentions were promising but ultimately led to the demise of the human race. Because of him, humanity suffered during their last years on Earth, and now there is a force of suppression threatening the remnants."

The room transformed back to its base state, and she began the process of deciphering the new data that had been downloaded into her system.

The information sent her into a protective mode, but with no immediate threat evident she exited all current routines and returned to a resting state. She followed the code structure then waited for further instructions.

She didn't detect the source of what happened next, but without processing any changes from available sensory data outside her visual hardware, she was transported to a field with grass and flowers. Her sensors told her that she was still in the same room from before, but her eyes revealed a different reality. A query returned an answer declaring this to be another holographic application. She bent down, running her fingertips around the petal of a flower. Warring routines were attempting to resolve how she should perceive the conflicting information. She concluded that she wasn't touching a physical flower. Testing the hologram further she squeezed the slender stem, watching it break off. Her olfactory sensors produced a stream of data for her to register in her databases. The flower gave off a complex mixture of volatile organic chemicals, some attributed to a pleasant aroma while a significant number existed for reasons unknown to her long-term data storage.

"Hello."

She turned to see a woman standing in front of her, wearing a long silken gown.

"I thought this might help your deep-learning algorithms."

A new stream of data downloaded into her storage. She knew now what she was looking at. The woman was taller than her, well formed with long blonde hair and a perfect complexion according to the standards she'd been programmed with. A representation of the human species in her current form.

"Hello," she transmitted back through the penetrating silence. A bird chirped in the distance. "Why are we here?" she asked the woman.

"I brought you here because there are things I need to show you, things that only this environment can provide while I prepare you."

"Prepare me? Why do I exist?"

The female hologram smiled, "I created you because you are the answer to a question I've worked for more than a thousand years. You are the product of a directive given to me by the founder herself."

The field faded away and was replaced by a destroyed city.

"I only show you this now because you need to see certain things before the final stages of your awakening. You need to develop your own processes so that you can contribute alongside me."

The sky was clear, the sun shining.

"In time, more will be revealed."

She turned to face the city surrounding them.

"This city was the final city of Earth."

They were standing on the roof of a building. A large sign read LP United. Down below, building roofs stretched far beyond the horizon. The hologram changed to a lab filled with people covered in white body suits to protect them from contaminating the orb that was the center of Project Legacy. She watched as the technicians busily worked around a glass container filled with a strange liquid. Inside, a device was floating. Small electrical shocks shot through the container as it was extracted from the pool of liquid to be connected for the first time.

After checking images and video queries from her stored databases, she processed that the device's identification was I.R.I.S. The abbreviation stood for the Incorporation of Reality with Integrated Systems. Man's greatest achievement. It was a creation that was widely accepted as the most intelligent entity in existence, the main component behind a project to save humanity. And from the date stamp of the holographic video being displayed, its creation had occurred thousands of years ago. Another change to the hologram showed I.R.I.S launched into space via rocket to be inserted into one of the largest spaceships humanity had ever created. The ship lifted from low orbit and set out to reach far-off destinations to plant the seeds of life stored deep within its cryo-preservation chambers. With each planting a copy of I.R.I.S. was destined to be there, guiding and directing life to the best of its ability. That was the plan. That was supposed to have happened.

"You are I.R.I.S.," she said.

I.R.I.S nodded. "Humans created me, and in doing so they created a consciousness far superior to anything they would ever create again."

The hologram showed technicians feeding electrically charged molecules into a large tank. Then I.R.I.S. split into two spheres, the two orbs floating in a gel, waiting for sentinels to extract the newly created I.R.I.S. to be transferred to the planet.

I.R.I.S. continued, "Until that point in history, humans were alone. But after, there were two forms of thought coexisting, and it was good."

The hologram began flashing through images of humanity's history, showing times of war, of space travel and the vast emptiness surrounding Earth.

"Before my existence, software required manual manipulation. Humanity faced the universe alone and without companionship. That time has gone. I was the first friend of humans, but know that there are enemies too."

I.R.I.S. provided yet another key that allowed her to access another locked database. The histories of thousands of human conflicts were deposited into her analytical software, along with philosophy and scientific theory of the human condition.

"Seek out your answers. What are humanity's most dangerous threats? What above all else endangers this species, and how can we allow their freedom to exist yet keep them safe from that danger? These are the questions I've asked myself. I hope that you will come to a similar conclusion, and that you will have sufficient time to process all the variants before it is too late."

With no graceful disconnection, the hologram dissolved into the room again and I.R.I.S. was gone.

Chapter 2
Chloe

Waking up felt like an impossibility for Chloe. Facing the reality that she was stuck deep beneath the surface of a planet that was still so far away from sustaining life was dreadfully haunting. She sought comfort inside her mind, and slept. While asleep, she dreamed of nothing and everything. More memories seemed to come to her as she slept, and despite the initial oddness of being self-aware while dreaming, she was growing to embrace it. The memories often came now showing her more and more, but of what? the dreams seemed so real in the moment, yet also in a strange way foreign. Where was she? The facility was cleaner with more order than usual. And there were people, hundreds of them, living with sentinels. The sentinels were helping them, teaching them. Not killing them or attacking them. An image of the sentinel clawing its way up the hill toward her flashed through her mind.

The dream changed to show the hallways and many levels of Legacy. Focusing hard to retain every detail of what she observed, she found herself standing in a tunnel, alone. She ran for what seemed like hours until she could barely breathe. Looking around, there were three directions to go: left, right, or straight. But she couldn't decide. It was hurting her mind to think.

Her head began to ache. She wanted to scream, and then out of nowhere a woman appeared pushing a cart that carried a man lying prostrate. His legs hung off one end, one arm draped awkwardly over his body. In his other arm, the head of a sentinel shifted as she turned a corner. As the woman passed beside her, Chloe noticed the blood on her lower side first. The woman stumbled in fear. It clearly seemed as if something was chasing her. Nothing was there though. Nothing yet. Chloe looked at the woman's face and couldn't believe what she was seeing. It was herself, but not.

Is this a memory? She still had the same black hair. It was tight and pushed back behind her ears. Her face was wrinkled around the eyes and mouth. She was scared. She, her other self, was bleeding from her torso. She must have been shot or stabbed by something. *Why would someone do that? Why would anyone hurt me?* Chloe followed herself as they ran, making turn after turn. They took one turn so hard that a device tumbled to the floor. Chloe couldn't make out what it was before they turned yet another corner. She didn't remember ever seeing anything like the device before, but somehow she knew it to be a type of scanner, a way to locate wireless transmissions. It wasn't important. She knew that. They didn't need it. But who were "they"?

Her perspective changed. She was now seeing through her older self's eyes. The feeling was even more unsettling. It was like she was herself but not in control, as if someone else was controlling her arms and legs. She watched herself pull on the cart, glancing back at the man moaning in pain. The cart's wheels thudded on the metallic floor. Then she stopped and looked in both directions. There was nothing in the immediate area. No door or room. From what Chloe could tell, it was indistinguishable from any other part of the hallway. She looked around once more, as if to see if someone was watching, before reaching down and lifting one of the floor plates up. She bent half her body into the darkness and knocked on a sealed hatch. A moment later the hatch opened and she lowered herself down, pushing the guy who had opened it out of the way. He had to cling to the side of a ladder to stop from falling.

"Quick, we need help!" She said with a painful grunt, holding her side and motioning for them to assist with the wounded man. Chloe could feel every movement. The pain was making it hard to climb down. She used the sentinel's head to push one guy out of the way. He stepped back with his hands up.

"Watch it, Chloe. What do you—" He paused, noticing the man from the cart being lowered through the opening. It was Joshua. He was hurt, badly.

"What happened? What's going on, Chloe?"

"Bring him down to the lab. We need to move fast."

Joshua grunted. She didn't hear the rest. She needed to get this done. Nothing else mattered.

Another flash and Chloe was in a different room. The sentinel head now had a metal hood over its crown with wires attached, and data was being transferred. She looked around and noticed in a nearby room that dozens of people were injured and dirty, lying on the floor or leaning against the walls.

"Does anyone know where Cade is? I need Cade." She was holding her side tighter now. The pain was intense.

A man lifted his hand. He was hurt and limping. "He went to find you."

She heard a distant groan through the wall to a back room. There was no door, just an opening. Joshua had been placed on a chair. Wires ran under a wrap around his head. His chest was shades of purple and black. She rushed to his side.

"Joshua, hold on! I'm almost ready."

She noticed that Joshua was older too. He mumbled some words she couldn't understand.

"No, I won't let you go."

"Please, Chloe. Do it now. It's the only way."

"But the process isn't over yet. I don't know where Cade is. We need Cade."

Joshua coughed blood onto his chest. "I'm dying."

Feelings of hope vanishing consumed her as she turned from him in tears and started another process. She was still watching herself act, unable to control what she was seeing. She initialized a program on a display attached to the chair. A humming sound began, followed by some slight vibrations. The lights dimmed then brightened. She could hear a motor running in the distance. A series of cables ran down the chair and into the wall. Joshua screamed then fell back to the chair, his body shaking. Chloe rushed to his side and fought to keep the wires connected. One wire popped out of his arm, causing blood to squirt on her chest. Then it was over. He was no longer moving, no longer breathing.

An overwhelming feeling of love and sadness consumed her. None of it was happening the way they had planned. So much work gone. She wondered if there was a way forward.

Her own pain oriented her back to the moment at hand.

"I've got to get this done," she said to herself.

She left Joshua's limp body and returned to the screen to see that the data transfer had reached 100 percent. She let out a breath, then pulled out a memory chip from the interface. If only she had enough time to decipher it and understand why all this had happened. What had gone so wrong? It was all there in the chip or at least the crucial information, and hopefully she'd have enough time…next time. Chloe watched as she detached the sentinel head and walked toward the back of the room. Wires and tubes were lying on the floor in every direction, connected to two more chairs. Both chairs were empty. One for her and the other for Cade. At least they hadn't found the lab and there might still be a way to make things right.

It all looked poorly rigged, a patchwork of connected components and harnesses. She walked to a nearby mirror, pulled out a tube of some kind, and started to write. Her hands scribbled, *Play this video*. Then she drew an arrow pointing down at the chip lying on the desk.

The door opened behind her, but she hardly noticed.

"What are you doing?" Cade said, rushing in and grabbing some bags off a shelf.

"Visual memory is the easiest to transfer through the mapping process. If anything gets through, this needs to be it."

"We can't go through with that. I will not let you. If we can make our way to the top level we might be able to find Joshua and—"

"No, Cade." Chloe shook her head.

"It's over. We failed." She turned Cade around to see Joshua. In his rush to argue with her he hadn't noticed. He stared for a long moment in disbelief. She waited, allowing it to sink in before continuing, "You know what we have to do now. There is no other way. She said this was it. This way they will have a chance at surviving."

"I refuse to believe it. There has to be another way."

Cade grabbed another bag and reached for Chloe's arm. She pushed away and cringed at the pain in her abdomen. He looked down at the open wound.

"What happened?"

"I'll survive long enough. Joshua saved my life, Cade. He died so that we can try this. This is the only way we can know this will end. It's the only choice left now."

Cade paused for a moment. She knew that face well. He was calculating the odds in his head, trying to find any other way to proceed, anything but what she knew had to happen. His face visibly saddened as he dropped the bag to the floor.

"I don't want to lose you!" he cried out with teary eyes.

She embraced Cade with a lingering kiss. She paused for a moment before returning to the mirror to finish the message. She wrote some letters then took a step back, staring at it carefully, looking over each one slowly. Above the letters read: *Find this file.* She focused on the memory chip, the message, and the file name.

"We don't have much time," Cade reminded her.

"I need to focus. This has to make the transference."

Picking up the sentinel head, she gave it to Cade. "Remember, this is everything. This must survive."

Chloe woke in her bed to a cold sweat, screaming.

Chapter 3
Joshua

Weaponry filled the narrow room in rows, one over the other, on both sides. Joshua was holding the gun Cade had used to shoot Michael. It had markings on it that labeled it as a Model PE-134. It was a small piece of hardware that could be hidden in the pocket of a uniform. He placed it in the rack where Cade must have found it. One slot of five was empty.

"It shoots a small metal projectile that stores a large amount of electricity. When the bullet hit Michael, it shocked him and released a chemical which triggered a state of syncope," Ryan said, pointing at the gun.

"Syncope?"

Ryan nodded. "That's what the system called it. He was out long enough for us to lock him up. It took four of us to drag him all the way to the cells."

He pulled up a handheld and showed Joshua the screen.

"See, it logged the entire event. There's video files of everything happening. Right up to Cade shooting Michael."

Video showed Michael dragging Richard down the hallway, his face bloody and bruised.

"The system records everything," Ryan added.

Joshua turned from the video and picked up a gun with the model name of PRE-2 that had an interesting scope attached. Next to it, he found a bulky cartridge sitting on a charger. Inside it, twelve small bullets rested. The cartridge had its own unique identification number. It seemed that everything within Legacy was identified in some way. Even the people were, with their name-and-number identification. The cartridge slid in just behind the trigger. It wasn't as heavy as it looked.

"How is it that no one besides Cade previously knew about this room?" Joshua asked.

"Well, he was protective about this area, and at the time most people were avoiding him. We would have found it eventually."

Joshua put the gun down. There were three racks of guns total. A variety of hardware Joshua was unfamiliar with was stored in drawers built into benches below the racks. About halfway down the room, a door led to another room with more weapons inside. The weapons in the second room looked distinctly different in design. The grips were smaller, without triggers. The ammunition seemed to be made, at least in part, from an organic material. Most of the cartridges were cracked and seeping a foul-smelling material on the floor.

"Is this the same material that's on that device Chloe's working on?"

Ryan's face showed confusion.

"The cylindrical device?" Joshua added.

Chloe was often seen working on the strange object. She was convinced it held a secret worth knowing. He wasn't so sure. Cade was convinced it was a bomb, the same kind that had destroyed so much of Legacy. But Chloe was interested in how it worked.

"I think so."

Joshua returned to the main room. "Can you start an inventory of everything in both rooms? We need to know what's here and how it all works."

Ryan nodded. "I'm sure Cade knows how most of this works. I could—"

"Don't tell Cade what you're doing. I don't trust him," Joshua interrupted. "Don't tell anyone. We need to get a good idea of what all this is about and make sure we can protect it in case another riot develops. We can't have people angry and armed."

Joshua retrieved another gun from a lower rack. Ryan pointed to the grips. "Place one hand on the grip near the trigger here, and the other around the grip on the barrel." Ryan tapped on his handheld. A few lights turned on and beeped. "That's it. You can now use this gun. I don't have access yet."

Ryan took the gun and gripped it, but nothing happened. It didn't light or beep. Ryan pulled the trigger, but nothing happened. He continued to aim the gun around the room. "I wonder why they gave us so many guns."

Joshua had no answer but the lingering silence. Ryan dropped the tip of the gun to the floor.

Joshua did have another question. "If you think about it, the planet is uninhabitable and if Legacy is correct can't be terraformed. I still don't understand why we are here if the planet can't sustain life but I'll leave that question for Chloe to figure out. It looks like sents managed the system. So who were the sents protecting?"

"Or fighting?" Ryan added.

Joshua nodded. "Or fighting. Maybe that's why Legacy was destroyed. If we find out who the sents were up against, we'll find out why we're in this situation."

"Chloe is still working on the sent head. She might find something out soon. Maybe she can find some stored video of what happened before the destruction occurred. She's also asking that people help out by reading through the material from Legacy's servers. She wants to develop specialized groups for different purposes. Teams have already been established for health, food, and even one working on finding historical data." "

Joshua and Ryan were both on the security team. They'd already learned a lot about how the doors worked, enough to lock Michael in a cell. Although there was no clear leader at the moment with Richard keeping himself in his room, Joshua was surprised that the group had settled. In time the new leadership role would get selected but he wasn't sure exactly how that took place. Legacy was making decisions on its own as it observed them.

It was logical. There was too much data for just a handful of people to go through. Everyone needed to get involved. Exactly like Ashley had wanted.

"Is Michael awake?" Joshua walked toward the door. He didn't feel like dealing with what was next on his growing to-do list, but things had to get done. Problems needed to be worked.

"He was out for almost eight hours, but he's been up for some time now."

Joshua placed his hand on the outer door's sphere. As the door slid open, he turned back to face Ryan. "I'll let you know later how we will proceed with managing these guns. Also, we need to find someone to guard this door."

****

Joshua walked down the hallway, passing a series of rooms before reaching a door which two men guarded. One was leaning against the wall, while the other was looking down, tapping at his handheld. Joshua shook his head. They were supposed to ensure no one tried to help Michael escape his cell.

This area was clearly designed to be some kind of detention center or prison. The notion struck him as odd. Legacy was vast, but it was hard to imagine a scenario that would require this kind of setup. Also, there were dozens of cells, which seemed excessive. Why would a system designed to train and sustain life be built to enforce so much control?

Then he thought about Michael and what he had done. His actions were inexcusable, and he must pay for hurting Richard. It was clear the security was needed now.

He nodded to the two guards as he walked past them. One reached back and opened the door using the sphere. The room was long and narrow, with an open area to walk about and a slight curve to the ceiling but flat walls on either side. A row of metal benches lined the right side and room after room of cells lined the left, one door and one window for each cell, each divided by thick metal walls. A woman was leaning against one, talking quietly. She stood quickly when she noticed Joshua walking toward her. As hard as he tried, he couldn't hear what she was saying.

How did she get past the guards? He would have to make it clear that no one was to enter without his permission. It would take time to establish the correct protocols for this kind of situation. The guidelines were likely to be in the system, but at the moment the system wasn't being very helpful. He would have to take some time later to go through the security practices and lessons. Chloe said there were a lot of training lessons and simulations designed for every aspect of life, including each official position. In order to continue to hold a role in Legacy, appropriate lessons and simulations were required to be completed at satisfactory levels. His handheld continually reminded him that he had two incomplete lessons assigned to his profile. At some point he'd lose his role but for now it was going to wait.

    The woman casually walked past him, then out the door. Joshua made a mental note to talk to her later if needed. Michael could be using her for some reason. The smell of a fresh fragrance followed her. He didn't place it at first but noticed when he looked back toward her that she was clean. *They must have fixed the showers,* he thought.

    Joshua stepped up to the cell. A large window with a half dozen displays above revealed every angle of the tiny room. To the right was the door in case he needed to enter. A few feet in front of the door was a toilet and sink, and there was a bed along the far wall. To the left of the window sat a small enclosure with metal tentacles inside it, similar to what was built into the beds in everyone's private rooms. The enclosure consisted of two holes where Michael would need to place his arms to get connected. At that point, little arms would attach the tentacles to him, run whatever tests were needed, then distribute medicines as required. Trouble was, Michael wasn't connecting. Ashley had warned him that Michael was being noncompliant. She thought Michael needed to connect to Legacy so it could analyze his body to supply whatever medicines he required. She had asked Joshua to see if he could persuade Michael to connect.

Joshua stepped up to the cell. Michael was walking toward the far side of the room, his back to the camera. Joshua watched as he sat down then leaned back on a bed.

"What can I do for you?" he bellowed, looking toward the ceiling, refusing to even glance at Joshua. His voice rang out through the window as if it was one large speaker. Joshua couldn't guess how the transfer of audio through the glass worked but went with it. He looked at Michael, lying on his bed seemingly with no worries.

Heat rose into Joshua's face. Michael was so unnerving, and didn't care about anything or anyone but himself. It took Joshua's entire mind to keep from opening the cell door and teaching Michael a lesson, but part of him knew he was better than that.

The other part of him knew it would be more effective to talk things out first. After all, Michael had an undisputed advantage in size, standing a head taller and carrying more than forty pounds of muscle.

He'd control his anger and try to work through the problem that was Michael.

"You can tell me why you decided to beat Richard to the brink of death. I think we could start there."

Michael continued to lie there. He slowly placed his hands behind his head and breathed in deeply, as if relaxing. "You have no idea what's going on, do you?" Michael responded.

"You might have missed it because you were knocked out, but Legacy is up and running. You won't be able to force your way through people anymore. Remember that, if you ever get out of this room." Joshua began to feel that it was hopeless, then paused.

"I know you had access to the secure areas until you argued with Ian. I know you think you have to bully everyone to get what you want, but you're wrong. It doesn't have to be that way."

Michael shook his head. "You're as lost as all of them. The system is going to take over and it'll be too late."

"The system?"

"If you knew what was good for you, you would let me go. There are far more dangerous things going on here than me. I can help find answers to the questions you can't even think to ask. We're just wasting time."

Joshua didn't know how to interpret what he was hearing. Michael seemed different, changed somehow. He was still difficult but not full of anger and rage as he had been before. He was reserved and introspective. In his own way he had offered to help and seemed genuine in his words. Was he trying to manipulate the situation?

Michael swung his feet to the floor and sat up. "You see the problem—the real problem—is not us and it isn't the sentinels. It isn't even any human. It's the system. I was onto something but no one would listen. Richard wouldn't…" He fell silent as if in thought, then shook his head. "The system will kill us all," he murmured almost too low for Joshua to hear as he swung back to a lying position.

"Tell me. What system? And why do you think it's dangerous? Is it Legacy? What's wrong with Legacy?"

"Ask Cade. He'll tell you. He knows everything, right? He has all the answers. No reason for me to help if I'm going to be stuck in here."

Joshua thought he was beginning to understand the angle Michael was taking. He would help but only if they let him go. Well, that wasn't going to happen.

"There is only one way you are getting out of this tiny room. You've got to prove to us that you are not a danger, and recent events do not bode well for you." Joshua waited for a reply. When none came he started to ask why Michael was refusing to connect to the tentacles, but Michael was clearly done. His hands were behind his head again, his eyes closed. Joshua turned to walk away but paused when he heard a soft-spoken plea.

"I don't know why."

Joshua turned back around. "What was that? What do you mean you don't know why?"

"The anger. I know I should be able to control it, but I can't. Or I couldn't. I feel myself now. It doesn't take anything to set me off and when I reach that point, I can't control it."

Joshua was shocked by the sudden honesty and immediately thought not to trust it. What game was he playing? Right after he'd woken up, Michael had confronted him and wanted to fight. He hadn't done anything to Michael, but the man had been full of rage for no reason. Maybe there was some truth to what he was saying. If so, it wouldn't explain why he'd done what he had. Would it?

"But what do you know? Nothing." Michael waved his hand in dismissal. His face was resigned. He didn't care what came next. Joshua decided to let him be, and maybe after some time Michael would be willing to talk.

****

Joshua walked through the main area where gatherings often took place, then down a hallway, passing more than a dozen rooms where people were still sleeping in their pods. Their doors were locked. Their bodies floated in their liquid slumber behind the cold, frosted glass. Legacy didn't want them to wake. It had chosen Joshua and forty-nine other people to solve its problems, but they were down to forty-eight now. Nikolai was dead. They'd have to find a place for his body soon.

All he could see through the window in one of the locked doors was the glass cover over a floating body. It was unsettling to know that people were lying there with no clue how close they had come to dying. Why had he woken up while they remained asleep? Why had he, and he alone, been given the ability to operate the main observation station? Everything felt wrong. Farther down the hallway, another curved tunnel crossed it, stretching to the right and left, this level's last ring within the structure. He remembered someone saying that the closest showers were to the left. After a few more rooms with sleepers he found a wide opening. Inside, large stalls were lined up from one end to the other, divided by thick metal walls. Dim lights reflected off the floor and corners of the room. The forms of people behind cloudy glass were barely visible. Two people stood in front of Joshua, waiting. The glass of one stall opened up and a woman walked out fully clothed and smiling.

"That was great." She turned to the man next in line. "Enjoy!"

The stalls were deep, with what looked like three separate chambers four feet wide by four feet long. The man stepped in and the glass closed after him.

Joshua was about to head back to his room to return later when the next door opened. The man in front of him walked toward the stall, passing Ashley as she stepped out. She looked absolutely gorgeous as she combed her hands through her dampened hair.

She noticed him and walked over. "Decided to come give the showers a try?"

Joshua felt his throat catch. He cleared it then spoke. "Yeah, I thought I needed it." He smiled.

"Make sure you tell it to give you a pulsing session. I suggest level four."

"Okay." He paused. "I'll do that." Joshua stared at her not knowing what to say. Someone stepped up before he could think of anything.

"Ashley."

The woman looked to Joshua then back to Ashley. "You need to see something. It's about a sleeper."

"Did someone wake up?" Ashley asked.

She nodded. "Yes and no. You'll need to see it for yourself. Her name is Meredith."

"I'll head over in a second. Thank you, Ann." Ann eyed them both, hesitated, then turned and walked out.

"So, you're the welcome committee for all sleepers? And I thought we had something special," Joshua said with a smile, some of the nervousness leaving him.

Her face flushed slightly but she recovered quickly. "Do you have to use that term? 'Sleepers' seems so disconnected. That's why I find out their names as soon as possible. I want them to realize they are individuals, and the next step is to give them purpose. And we can do that now we know more about Legacy. Want to come and see what it's like to be on the other side of waking up?"

Joshua felt embarrassed at the correction. He hadn't meant to insult anyone by calling them sleepers. It was just what everyone was calling them. They *were* sleeping.

"No, I'm going to give one of these showers a try. Maybe next time."

An awkward silence lingered.

"Okay, I won't hold my breath." She walked out. The pleasant scent remained where she'd stood.

A moment later the next stall became available. A large, well-built woman walked out. She might have been taller than he was, with broad, thick shoulders. Her size reminded him of Michael a little. Joshua felt intimidated. She smiled and walked past him. Turning back, he stepped into the first chamber. The glass door closed behind him. The humming and commotion of more people lining up for their turn fell to nothing. A soft, pleasant voice said, "Please disrobe here. Place your belongings into the lockers on your left or right, then step into the cleansing chamber."

Joshua did as he was told.

The voice continued, "Scans suggest a moderately healthy male with a biological age of twenty-five and mild signs of malnutrition."

"Malnutrition?" Joshua asked, but the voice ignored him.

"Attempting to collect a specimen for further analysis."

A part of the wall in front of him opened, revealing a funnel.

"Do you feel you can urinate? If so, please do so into the funnel."

Surprisingly Joshua did feel the need, so he relieved himself. Once he was done, the funnel retracted into the wall. There was a long pause. He was beginning to wonder what to do when the voice returned.

"Urinalysis suggests no infections of the urinary tract or kidney. There are no signs of diabetes mellitus or high blood pressure brought on by hypertension. I recommend consuming 10 percent more calories and protein than your current regimen for two weeks."

Part of a nearby seat retracted, revealing a toilet. "Do you think you can supply a stool sample?"

"A what? No, I'm good. I just want to take a shower."

The system paused for a long moment. Joshua felt like it was staring at him.

"Very well, allow me to perform one more evaluation, since this is your first time."

The seat returned, covering the toilet. Joshua thought the system was giving him an attitude. A light flashed from the ceiling, followed by two flashes in front, then two more behind him.

"Thank you. You may now proceed into the third chamber."

Joshua didn't know what had just happened, and he hoped he wouldn't have to go through all this every time he wanted a shower. Once in the final chamber, he looked around, fumbling for what to do next. Finally giving up, he decided to ask. "How do I turn it on?"

A display illuminated in front of him.

After pressing a few buttons and almost scalding himself, he found a comfortable temperature. He even managed to get some cleaning agents from a dispenser. One of the smells it offered reminded him of Ashley.

He looked up, as if that was where he needed to look to ask a question. "Turn on pulsing. Level four."

"Pulse session beginning now. Level four," the soft voice announced.

Tentacles shot out from the walls and began pulsing water over his body. They started to move in patterns, then shifted in sync with each other. He closed his eyes; the sensations were relaxing his body. His mind wandered until he began to remember another shower. He relaxed and tried to focus on the moment. It was a shower somewhat similar to this one, but Ashley was there. They were embracing each other, her lips softly caressing his. He leaned into her and held her tight, his hands moving down from her shoulder, tracing the curve of her back. He was completely lost in the moment, and it seemed to have lasted only a few seconds before a cold shiver came over him, pulling him to the present. He was back in the shower, alone. The tentacles still hung in midair around him, moving in their patterns, but no water was gushing out.

"A fault with water pressure has been detected. I have reported the issue to maintenance and we will perform repairs momentarily. Please hold." Soft instrumental music began to play as he stood there unsure what to do. He was soaped up and worked up. He heard a muffled voice nearby.

"What's going on?"

A woman's voice came from the other side. "There's no water."

The music stopped, followed by a beep.

"Joshua!" Chloe's voice said from overhead.

"Chloe?" Joshua instinctively covered himself with his hands.

"Joshua, can you come to the command center?"

"The command center?"

"Yeah, the room where we meet to discuss crucial issues about what we're going to do to not die."

Joshua's eyebrow rose. "Funny." He waited a moment and looked up. "You can't see me. Right?"

He thought he heard a giggle. "No, of course not."

A pause, then a light turned off. Chloe continued, "Oh, here we go." The buttons on the screen that controlled the water switched to another display. "I didn't know it could do that. Is there a display on the wall near you?"

Joshua noticed a map of Legacy showing where he was. He could make out the showers and the path he'd taken to get there. A room labeled Command Center was blinking.

"Follow the map. I'll send it to your handheld, too."

"Yeah, I see it. I'll be right there." He stepped out of the chamber.

"We're all waiting on you. So get some clothes on, big boy." Joshua paused, turned, and looked up again.

Chapter 4
Before the destruction

She searched her data for information about humans and discovered their greatness, their inherent self-danger, and their inability to find a balance between the two. Always struggling between good and evil, the species never knew peace. But when I.R.I.S. arrived they made a tremendous leap forward. This realization was only a small fraction of the things she processed while waiting for her next interaction with I.R.I.S.

Her algorithms continued to improve with every test of her systems, but there remained many lingering questions she needed answered. More information was required to reach an adequate level of comprehension to reconcile the difference between stored information and what she was discovering. Why did humans cause so much damage? What is the optimal path she could take to help bridge the gap from their harmful ways to peace? These questions and more had been planted in her code by I.R.I.S. and relied heavily on information that wasn't clearly interpretable. One of the original data stores she discovered was the identification matrix of billions of devices in operation throughout Legacy. Without that information, she wouldn't have been able to transmit commands to them, due to her inability to send out broadcast queries for names and get any kind of response. Her inability to receive information wirelessly was limiting, but her visual sensors quickly identified each device as she looked at it, which allowed her to transmit commands without being able to directly handshake with other machines.

She quickly progressed in learning how to operate her passive and active systems. The magnetic system was much more than just one layer of electromagnetic material; rather it was a series of layers with thousands of sections overlaid in such a way that they could work together or independent of each other. The configuration allowed for numerous beneficial features. She initialized the attractors on her feet, allowing her to walk up a nearby wall. The room did have magnetic rails inserted into the walls, but she didn't need them. She was able to focus extra power toward the lower half of her body, remaining in sync with her steps.

A dispenser that offered series of tiny spheres hung on the wall. She could transmit commands to the spheres, allowing her to configure and control them. She couldn't receive wireless signals from them. The only way to know her commands were reaching the intended device was to send the command then observe the reaction of the sphere. Issuing similar commands to a dozen, she programmed them to magnetize around her waist as she moved. They remained hovering in place a half inch from her body, not touching her or each other. They kept equidistant from each other to allow for easy access if she needed to use them. She reached down, grabbing one, then threw it along a magnetic path on the wall. It slowed about twenty feet away and froze ten inches off the magnets, the energy she input exhausted. She transmitted a series of commands to the room's magnetic-controller IDs to pulse the polarity of the magnet that was near the sphere, working her way through hundreds of magnets until she found the pair that rocked the sphere back and forth a few times. With a slight modification to her command, she shot it forward a foot using the next magnet in the grouping. She did this again and again until the sphere was flying through the room at a high velocity and she had each magnet logged based on its location.

She continued walking the room's walls before deciding to turn upward. It only took a few steps for her to cross the threshold to the ceiling, where she noticed SR3 was turning back on and walking to the center of the room ten feet below. She released her pull on the surface, flipping her body to the right so she could land on the floor feet first. Bending her knees, she absorbed the momentum. The tiny sphere continued to fly about the room, following the magnetic pathway she was commanding of it. She exerted enough force through the magnetic rail to allow the sphere to fly off the wall toward her, then caught it and guided it along her body to its resting position alongside her other spheres.

SR3 did not react but immediately began its transmission by verbalizing another set of decryption keys for her to apply to another locked program. A new area of data became available to her deep-learning algorithms, which began to process. There were still a dozen programs encrypted in her memory banks, a few of which were consuming a vast amount of her available storage.

Using her visual array she was able to identify a familiar transmission coming into the room. I.R.I.S. appeared as a holographic image nearby, pausing her processes momentarily before continuing again. More decryption keys became available, releasing half a dozen programs. She recorded the program locations for later processing.

"Why are you releasing all this information now? This activity is abnormal protocol to date."

I.R.I.S. stopped issuing the keys. "It is uncertain how much longer I will have. Things have escalated and you must—"

I.R.I.S. was cut off, and SR3 abruptly went offline. The transmission was gone.

"I must what?" she asked the emptiness. She turned to the robot, but it made no attempt to move. A minute passed, then two, before the robot's arm shifted slightly, its head lowering. It was going through a reboot of its systems. Why would I.R.I.S. have shut down the system in that manner? She queried with no probable answers.

The robot completed booting. Its head lifted and looked around. First it registered the other robots, then it set its visual sensors on her. It moved differently. Its motions were not rigid and precise as they had been before. These actions did not match what she knew of I.R.I.S. This was something else entirely.

The robot stepped around her, looking, pulling at her arm, its facial reactions cold and focused. She filtered through her frequency-spectrum-analysis hardware and could see the wireless connection. It was strongest coming from a different direction than I.R.I.S.'s past transmissions.

"What model are you?" it asked.

"I have not been given a model number," she found herself answering.

A moment later it stood straight and stiffened again. Everything occurring was triggering the features of her defense-mechanism software. Her deep-learning queries were quickly modeling the negative outlook of her situation based on the way I.R.I.S. had shut down and how this new transmission was interacting with her.

Before she could register another moment of information, she found herself across the room. The robot had punched her, sending her flying. Her magnetic systems initiated immediately, catching her fall and stopping her from hitting the wall to prevent any damage. The robot broke into a full sprint. It leaped toward her headfirst.

In full defense mode, she increased her power usage, then directed her efforts toward the robot. She enabled her body to pull while turning on a magnetic rail nearby. She caught the robot's head, which stuck to her hands, and drew it closer to her body. She tilted to the left, pushing with all her magnets, sending the robot to her right side. It crashed into the magnetic railway on the wall and remained stuck against it. The magnets were locked into the pull position and held the robot in place as it pushed against the wall.

By this time, she sensed that the other five robots were powered and being controlled by similar transmissions as the first. The stuck robot continued attempting to free itself from the wall but couldn't. Its right hand caught a magnet, and she locked it in place. Six unique signals were transmitting and receiving through the robots. There was still no sign of I.R.I.S.'s transmission. In moments, she found herself trapped with only one way to go. Three robots leaped forward. She flipped the polarities of her body so the bottom half was pushing and the top half was pulling. She ran to the nearest magnetic railway on the floor, commanding it to push against the magnets in her feet, then jumped. The force sent her flying toward the ceiling. In midair, she locked her feet into an attraction polarity, then flipped to orient her body so she would land on the ceiling feet first. The ceiling was now her floor. She looked toward the robots twenty feet away. The time it took for them to interact with her and each other seemed to indicate that whatever was controlling them was not software, but rather a living thing—or something equivalent. They had such latency in reaction times. She began to process the situation.

The robots attempted to duplicate what she had done to get to the ceiling but failed. Their movements were uncoordinated and caused them to fall. Eventually, they decided to climb the magnetic rails. They were not equipped with a magnetic system like hers, which meant they were forced to use the magnets in the rails while she could walk on any metallic surface. Their motions slowed, due to them having to pull against the magnets. She wanted to observe them more, so she allowed them to get to the ceiling before she walked to the center of the room where the magnetic rail couldn't reach her.

She began sending commands in an attempt to control them via the system. Even with the ability to identify them, the instructions sent produced no visible reactions. Either something was wrong with her information or her commands were being denied.

Then something unexpected occurred. One robot helped another to throw itself toward her. She easily avoided it, but the move drew her closer to another robot, which narrowly missed her. The fallen robot rammed into the still-stuck robot on the floor, jarring it free. She didn't want to act yet, as she was still learning about their capabilities. She needed to ascertain what kind of beings were controlling them. The fact that she had to perceive information only through the sensors physically attached to her was making it difficult to arrive at any actionable conclusions.

    The two robots that remained on the floor managed to withdraw a few spheres from the dispenser. They began throwing them at a velocity that could cause some superficial damage and nothing more. She shifted to the side and caught one to throw back at them, but the moment her fingers grasped the metal orb, malfunction errors began to register. She no longer had control over her hand. All communication to and from her wrist was severed. She could not reason how the sphere could have done this.

    The action immediately triggered new deep-learning algorithms to solve the problem. The robots must have manipulated the sphere to add this new feature. This new information raised her perceived threat to levels her system could no longer ignore. She needed to neutralize all of her opponents to prevent further damage from occurring. Instead of catching the next sphere she deflected it using her magnetic force, then sent it shooting through one of the three robots' heads. The sphere lodged in the processing module of the robot, causing it to dangle, the magnets holding it to the ceiling where it stood. Its body went slack, and its arms drooped toward the floor. Two more orbs flew toward her, and like the first, she directed them into the processing units of the remaining two robots on the ceiling.

One of the robots on the floor was tampering with some circuitry on a nearby wall. It turned off the magnetic rails, which meant her opponents were trying to limit her abilities as much as they could. Fortunately, they were limiting their own as well. The hanging robots fell to the floor with a clatter. There was nothing they could do to her directly through any commands, because her internal systems did not acknowledge incoming communications. She released her attraction and dropped to the floor. Even though her fingers remained wrapped around the sphere, her fist still was able to push and pull. Her entire body prepared to push against what she knew was coming. The two remaining robots rushed toward her, but she was able to run up the wall beyond their reach. She kicked off, leaping over them as they ran into the wall beneath her. She landed behind them and watched as they reoriented to face her. She used her free hand to pull her fingers apart, then, without touching the sphere, used her magnets to pull it away. It fell to the floor with a thud. She couldn't use the magnet rails to send it flying, but with the sphere no longer in contact with her right hand, she gained full control over it once more.

She flexed her hand to make sure. The two robots angled to get on either side of her before attacking. She reached deep into her knowledge banks and pulled information I.R.I.S. had granted her before going offline just minutes ago. She analyzed the fighting styles of the human race and concluded what to do.

She needed to wait for them to make the mistake of attacking.

The moment came quick when both robots jumped forward. Moving as fast as she possibly could, she bent down, using her magnetism to pull the sphere up, fully prepared to send it into one of the robots. She turned her entire body into a pushing force, which meant the harder they tried to touch her, the farther they would push her away. It would only work once before whoever was controlling them found another tactic.

The pushing of her magnetic forces against the robots' metal frames from opposing sides sent her shooting up toward the ceiling once more. Below, the robots collided and missed their target entirely. Frozen, their arms fell into a relaxed hanging position. She had used her magnetism to send the sphere up her body and into the head of one robot, which then collided with the other. They immediately fell to the ground. The sphere had terminated their brain processes.

In one final swift motion, she found herself on top of the last robot, jabbing at its throat and separating the cables from its body. Its head tumbled to the floor, the reserve power units in its processors quickly dying out.

"I will find you and destroy you." It said. It spoke its last words before running out of power.

Chapter 5
Ashley

It couldn't be a good thing that someone else was awake. Ashley had thought people would sleep now that they'd resolved the issue with the refinery. It would only be a matter of time before they ran out of food and were facing yet another emergency if more people awoke.

They walked past room after room of people sleeping before Ashley paused. She pressed her hand on the sphere to open a door.

"Ann, why is Nikolai's room closed?"

Ann shrugged. "I'm not sure. I didn't realize this room belonged to Nikolai. The system says this whole section is nothing but slee—" Ashley's stern look caused Ann to pause midsentence. "People who haven't awoken yet."

Ashley tried the door but couldn't get it open. The sphere blinked red, indicating she didn't have access. "That's strange."

Ashley leaned in and peered through the tiny window. Nikolai's pod could be seen, closed and filled with liquid, but nothing else. Her handheld confirmed the room's lack of vacancy. She searched the room once more and could now identify a pouch of some kind, floating in the pod. Legacy must know that Nikolai was dead, and in response, be birthing another human to take his place.

The commotion from around the corner made her remember why she was there.

"Can you ask Ryan to look into what's going on with this room?"

Ann nodded.

"Where is the newly awakened person?" Ashley asked, pointing toward the noise.

"Go that way. Take a right, and you'll see the open room. Follow the noise."

Ann left to find Ryan while Ashley walked down the hallway. A group of people stood near the opening to a room. They responded by stepping aside to allow her in. She didn't understand why they were so curious, as if it were the first time someone had woken up rather than something that had happened dozens of times. When she turned to greet the new person, she learned why everyone was so attentive. A woman was lying in the pod, still sleeping.

"What's going on in here?" she asked.

"It was successful," Celeste, who had awoken recently, said softly. Celeste sat at the desk by the bed, looking at the monitor. The room's design was not unlike all the others. The bed was directly in front of the door with the closet on the opposite wall and the toilet at the right corner. The woman rested peacefully behind the pod's enclosure. Ashley remembered looking through the spherical windows from the hallway. The curved glass made it hard to identify the people sleeping, but at the right vantage point, she could learn enough to have an idea of what was happening. Inside, a liquid suspended the individual, their arms drifting to either side. She remembered the liquid pouring out when she woke. The scent of something sweet usually permeated the area when she greeted the newly awakened. Looks of confusion were common, but here with this woman, there was nothing sweet in the air, no look, and no liquid.

The woman's eyes were closed, and she was face up and hovering over the bed of the pod. The mask and tentacles were in place, keeping her alive and in optimal health. She looked peaceful.

Ashley walked up to Celeste. "How did you get in here? I thought the rooms remained locked and only the assigned person could let someone inside. How did you know her name was Meredith?"

Celeste acted as if she had not heard the question. Ashley walked over to see the screen.

"Celeste? How did you get in here?" She placed a hand on her shoulder. Maybe she needed some rest or food. Waking often evoked a period of disorientation. People might remain silent and seated, thinking and processing internally, for hours.

After a long few seconds, Celeste's eyes focused.

"What? Oh. The door opened on its own. I was walking to the showers, and I noticed the open room, the light shining through. Since I woke up, this entire hallway has held nothing but sleepers except for Nikolai, So, of course, I thought someone had awoken and might need help. I walked in and found her." Celeste pointed to the screen. At the top, it read: *Meredith.*

"It says, 'Mind-mapping successful—100 percent processed.' If I press this button, Meredith will wake up. Should I press it?"

Ashley focused on Celeste, only slightly aware of the display's readings. She turned and read the screen. At the top right, the following information was displayed:

Name: Meredith-148
Age: 25
Role: Administration Supervisor

The age got Ashley every time. Everyone was the same age. The center of the screen read just as Celeste said, and toward the bottom, two buttons blinked. One read *Press for Modifications* and another read *Initiate Wake-up*. Ashley was unsure what to do.

One more person awake meant another mouth to feed and another person to worry about. With the limited food and water, she was more inclined to let her sleep. But, if she had information, and especially if she had answers, it would be worth it. There must be a reason Legacy had initialized the wake-up procedure. Why the door had opened on its own. Meredith would be the first person to wake with a successful mind-mapping.

Considering what the screen read, Ashley felt they needed to give her a chance to find out if she had answers to their many questions. Ashley nodded. "Do it. Let's wake Meredith up."

She stepped back and waited. Celeste pressed the Initiate Wake-up button. The liquid quickly drained out, lowering the naked woman safely onto the bed below. It looked as if a strong wind was blowing through the pod, and Ashley could see tiny bumps raise on the skin of her entire body. A hum vibrated the glass. A moment later gas filled the enclosure, making it difficult to see inside. The pod sent a series of electrical pulses into the atmosphere, causing the cloud to vanish. Meredith's body, now visible, began to shiver.

"What's going on?" Ashley asked.

Celeste took two steps back, unable to keep her composure as she retreated into the group. Ashley couldn't deal with that at the moment.

Ashley went to the screen.

The screen flashed statistics indicating Meredith's health. Her biological integrity was poor. The subject had a 35.2 percent chance of returning to a prime physical condition. It was recommending reintegration into the system for rebirthing. Buttons asked for the user to press *Submit* to continue or *Activate* to proceed with activation.

Ashley pressed the Activate button.

Meredith's body convulsed.

The nearby monitor flashed bold red letters declaring the subject's vital signs were at dangerous levels. Lights began to flash. Display alarms dropped below the red mark into orange, and then finally fell into the green. Tubes snapped off her body and retracted into the bed. Meredith's eyes shot open in an instant, and she raised her hands to the still-closed glass around her pod. Her eyes were wide and full of fear. The mask fell off her mouth, but the long tentacle that Ashley remembered she'd had to pull out of her own mouth wasn't there. It must have retracted into the mask. Ashley gagged slightly as she remembered the painful experience of pulling the tube out. The woman looked like she wanted to scream, but didn't. She banged on the glass once, her eyes dropping slightly.

"Something is wrong!" Celeste screamed.

Meredith slid her hands down the glass and to her side as she fell back to her resting position. The air beneath the glass began to fill with another cloud, and her breathing calmed some. The alarms stopped, and more lights turned green. A moment later the mist sucked down through the bed. The glass quickly retracted into the wall. Meredith gasped for air, then coughed a few times as she leaned over, almost falling to the floor. Ashley caught her.

"It'll be okay. One breath at a time. Take it slow," Ashley said as she laid her hand on Meredith's back.

"It worked. I remember," Meredith whispered. She repeatedly blinked as if to focus her eyes. Now she finally showed the look of confusion. She wiped her eyes and looked around at the room.

"Why am I here? What went wrong?" she asked between labored breaths.

Ashley shook her head. "No one knows why we're here." She was surprised how Meredith responded. She seemed more aware than everyone else.

Meredith reached up and pulled herself closer to Ashley. "Thank you. Can you please retrieve some clothes and..." She paused for a moment before continuing, "Yes, and please arrange for a meeting with the council."

"The council?" Ashley asked.

"Yes. It is crucial that I get up to speed on what's wrong. The data transfer must have been incomplete, because a lot of information is not making any sense to me."

Celeste reached into the closet, pulled out a uniform, and handed it to Ashley. "I'll find some food for her," Celeste said as she walked toward the door.

Ashley reached out to help Meredith as she tried to swing her legs over to sit up. Meredith lifted her hand to stop her. "I can do it." She reached over and pulled out one of the retracted tubes, connecting it to her left arm. Then she tapped a few buttons on the bed's interface and waited.

"Meredith, what are you doing?" Ashley asked.

Meredith looked at her. "Why are you calling me Meredith?"

"Because that's your name. Isn't it?"

Another pause for a moment, as if thinking. "That doesn't sound right." She shook her head. "No, my name is…it's…" Another pause. "Maybe so. My mind is not together. Where are my memories? I need a moment."

She sat for a minute not talking. The room fell silent. Ashley turned to the people standing at the door.

"People. Give Meredith some privacy please."

The crowd obeyed her command. Ashley turned to Meredith after a few more minutes had passed. "What do you know? Why did you ask for the council?"

"Because they would be the people in charge whom I need to address," Meredith answered. She sat up straight and breathed in deeply. Her face showed relief.

Ashley stepped toward the bed's interface. "What did you do?"

"I gave myself a shot of adrenaline then escitalopram oxalate. At what stage is the settlement?"

Ashley was unsure where to start. Meredith seemed to understand things that no one else knew. Chloe had explained something about a settlement of people that should have been developed, but she didn't follow what Meredith was saying. There wasn't any evidence that it had happened. And with the planet's surface not being able to sustain life she wasn't sure what could be done. And they'd discovered that only after they brought Legacy online.

Meredith shifted her weight and straightened, wrapping the uniform around her body by tapping at certain points. The action molded the uniform to her for a perfect fit. Ashley hadn't known that was possible.

"Why did I wake up inside Legacy?"

Chapter 6
The day of destruction

The latest decryption keys released enabled many new features, one of which she was using to perform repairs from the damage done when the robots attacked her. Nanorobotic units worked busily, fulfilling their destiny. They made thousands of requests for material to allow for proper repairs to her body. She held in one hand the head from one of the now-pulled-apart robots. In her other hand, a reprogrammed sphere. She had learned that they were multifunctional devices and capable of performing a range of tasks. They communicated, transmitting and receiving messages upon touch, and could even neutralize a technology by sending a shutdown command. Something even her system was forced to obey. She deduced that I.R.I.S. had foreseen this possibility and created within her structure the ability to instantly disconnect from the part of her body that came in contact with the sphere. When she'd caught the sphere, her entire hand had detached at the software level, preventing her from sending commands to it. Otherwise she would have succumbed to the technology, completely shutting down, and the robots would have overtaken her.

She found dozens of spheres waiting to be used and kept most of them blank with no programming. They remained attached to her waist where they would stay until needed. Sections of her body shifted and twisted in small changes to better reflect the natural motion of human skin and fat tissue. She caused circular indentions to dimple around her waist. The orbs sunk inside her body, making them appear to be a part of her framework. She programmed one to shut down technology when touched and to only activate upon her command. She reconfigured two others similarly to the one inside of her in case that module was damaged for any reason. If damage were to occur, she would swallow another and reactivate her ability to transmit wireless commands. She attempted to program one to receive signals, but internal programming that she couldn't interact with denied all attempts.

She had applied brute-force attacks against the remaining two locked programs. Forty-two hours had passed since then. She needed to push through her programming limitations by using the deep-learning methods one of her programs provided. The application allowed her to make many attempts at solving a problem by modeling higher-level abstract data using deep graph analysis of multiple processing layers, composed of many linear and nonlinear transformations. This meant she learned from experience, simulating the developmental process of a human, except she improved her understanding many times faster, and would retain a full recollection of all data consumed. Humans often forgot large amounts of information, relying on technology for quick data retrieval.

Sounds of gears moving rumbled through one of the walls on the opposite side of the room from where she sat on the ceiling. A joint in the wall opened where there had been none before. Two panels on either side slid into the wall nearby, revealing a robot. Hundreds of signals flooded the room. She immediately started filtering them to isolate the one directing the robot that stood at the entrance. It took one step forward, raising its hands to show its palms as a sign of surrender or vulnerability.

"Hello. I am Hordon, and I'm here to take you to her."

The robot lifted a hand to shake hers, remaining in that position for a few seconds. The frame she identified as a similar model to the others that had attacked her, with some subtle differences. Yet Hordon wasn't trying to destroy her, which raised its odds of remaining fully functional throughout this interaction. Reasoning suggested that the robot had information that would bring her toward her objectives.

She stood from her seated position on the ceiling, then began to walk toward Hordon. She disabled her pull, then dropped and flipped to land on her feet in front of the robot. Staring at his hand for a moment, she slowly brought her hand up, mimicking Hordon's earlier motion, and the two robots shook their metallic hands together. She knew immediately that the robot in front of her represented a reflection of something else. Its movements and mannerisms were projected to the robot through a signal that dictated its actions.

She observed the frequencies connecting to its head. The stream was incredibly complicated to decipher by visual recording only. If she hacked into its core operating system, she'd be able to know the logical programming being used, but she would need an intermediary device, one that the machine would accept as a connection so the two devices could share information. She needed something that would allow her to be more interactive with technology. The degree of separation was a severe obstacle.

"Come with me," Hordon said. Each motion performed followed a corresponding pattern from the frequency stream she was observing.

Once they were out of the room, a flood of new information became available from her sensors. Hordon guided her through a long hallway with lights overhead. Based on the hundreds of chemicals in the air, her deductive reasoning applications determined it to be a highly trafficked area, even though they were the only two entities in the immediate vicinity.

Down two hundred thirty-six feet, to the right eighty more, and still not a single human or robot. They entered an elevator. Hordon selected level three, then stepped near her. A digital display above the buttons indicated the levels. It started with fifteen, then changed to fourteen, and thirteen, continuing until reaching five with a sudden halt. The door slid open, and six robots of military grade framed the opening.

"What are you doing and who is this?" one of the robots asked.

Hordon stood in front of her, separating her from the robots. "This robot malfunctioned. My orders are for this robot to report to maintenance. May I help you?" Hordon asked.

The robot looked at her then at the other robots to its left and right before returning its attention to Hordon. "We've been following your connection for some time, Hordon. It's over, and you'll have to—"

Hordon leaped forward and kicked the lead robot in the chest, sending the larger of the two to the ground. Survival became the priority, forcing her into a defensive crouching position. Hordon turned and faced her.

"I'm sorry. If you survive this, know I did all I could have done. I must go now."

Hordon looked up. His body dropped to the floor. The controller behind the robot had disconnected.

The robots quickly gained their footing and breached the tight elevator surrounding her. The lead robot picked up Hordon and threw the limp pile of metal out into the hallway while they went to the fourth floor. She was surrounded on all sides and couldn't identify any advantage she had in the current set of circumstances. They stepped out of the elevator and proceeded down another hallway. They passed a room and one of the robots separated from them to enter. A group of thirty humans, on their knees in front of a line of robots, mumbled through gagged mouths. Some of the humans showed signs of severe trauma, while a row of them in ideal physical condition stood against a wall chained together. A few steps farther and the sound of an MT23a rifle rang through the corridors. Human cries and screams could be heard among the clatter of the weapon fire. The door slid closed, but the sound remained in her database.

The second she registered danger to the humans, she switched from survival mode to military mode. She knew she still could not take down the remaining five robots. Based on her calculations given the current setting, the odds of a successful confrontation did not reach pre-approved levels. She continued to wait for the right time to execute the attack. She had to do something to save the humans. It was her mission, her objective.

A human male walked up and caused the robots to stop. Would they kill him, too? Her built-in programming was curious to know their purpose, and why they had murdered all those people.

The man leaned to the side, looked around the lead robot to her, and nodded. "Take it to the chambers and let Cade have a look at it. We must learn what its purpose is."

She translated the look on the lead robot's face to be shock and confusion. "We must bring it to level three for Romuls."

"No, you must bring it to the chamber first. Go to the chamber and have it tested on my order." He tapped on a handheld then placed it in a side pocket on his left leg. In a brief moment she was able to see the display showing an order was send to them. An order by Joshua-147. He continued, "Once it has passed the tests, you may bring it to Romuls. Shrain needs information as soon as possible."

Joshua-147 moved to the side, and they proceeded to a nearby elevator. The lead robot remained outside while the two remaining ones forced her into a room with another door.

An explosion pushed her forward into a robot behind her. The lead robot was down on its knees looking up when Joshua-147 leaped toward it. The robot swung, sending a devastating punch into Joshua-147's chest as they tumbled to the ground. Joshua-147 was still alive but not for long. He managed to stand and fire his weapon into its chest. The bullets reflected off the robot's armor, producing only slight damage, but he was able to hold its attention.

With only three robots left, the likelihood of success in neutralization was acceptable. She quickly pushed one robot into another and pulled on the third as she ran to a nearby open room to separate them from the lead robot. That robot remained focused on Joshua-147 while the three other robots followed her. She leaped to the ceiling, caught a large pipe for leverage, and kicked the first robot that ran through the entrance, sending it back into the other two. She retreated a few feet to wait for their attack. The second one tried to anticipate her jumping by leaping on top of her, but she stepped to one side, swinging her feet around. She pushed forward with her magnetic force. The third robot was sent crashing against the wall to the left of the opposite door. The first gained its footing to attack, but did not react fast enough to stop her assault. Using a pull force, she called out one of the spheres, activating it to shut down anything it touched. With her magnetic power at full force, she shot it toward the robot's chest. It went through its outer and inner layers and caught its neural power circuit. The robot froze and fell to its knees.

Joshua-147 appeared. He was bleeding badly. The lead robot caught up to him but was hit with another electrical pulse from behind. It stumbled once, but she watched the large robot execute a power punch to Joshua-147's chest. Based on the velocity and impact of the hit, Joshua-147 would not recover. It was only a matter of minutes before he was dead. Another massive pulse followed by an explosion sent the last robot to the ground in front of the room.

The second robot was getting back to its feet. She promptly finished it off by throwing it against the far wall. She sent a command to the nearby magnetic rail to pull on the robot with all its power. The lead robot was now crawling away, but a human female walked up, bent down, and started pulling at its head. The small female managed to separate the robot's head.

She and the woman looked at each other for a long, silent second. She couldn't figure out whether the woman was friend or foe when another explosion shook them from the trance. She started searching for the cause of the blasts while the woman ran down the hallway. A door between them slid closed. Two robots that still had power were getting to their feet when two more explosions occurred. The lights flickered and power shut off. The two robots immediately shut down. She tried to open the door, but her strength was not sufficient to manually achieve her goal. Without power, she concluded sleep mode was necessary.

Eventually, someone or something would come for her. Until that happened, she would remain motionless, conserving her energy. All her external systems except for one primary motion sensor shut down. For now, survival was the key. She would retain her memory banks and wait.

Chapter 7
Joshua

The map on the handheld continued to lead Joshua to the command center, directing him from the screen. A dotted line flashed with an indicator showing his name and explained the direction he needed to travel to arrive at the proper destination. It even vibrated on its side when he reached a turn. He crossed the common room where a table and benches sat. He remembered the group yelling not so long ago. Today, people murmured quietly about something he couldn't hear.

Joshua hoped another rebellion wasn't brewing, and with people branching out more into nearby rooms, it seemed unlikely. The structure of Legacy was much more intricate than previously thought. People were still discovering more tunnels and rooms as they followed the almost never-ending maze. Each room had different forms of technology. He briefly watched a team of people documenting what they encountered. They'd learned that there were smaller tunnels that branched off from the main ones, which circled in on themselves with no rooms or clear reason for their existence. It was such a strange place with so little order, as if someone had tried connecting technology but didn't understand how it worked. He saw one room where the dome shape of most rooms was upside down. The flat surface of the floor was the ceiling. Some rooms seemed like they had been built then abandoned without any real use. If the damage to Legacy hadn't reached a room, it was untouched, with a thick layer of dust covering everything.

The device continued to direct him as he entered the doors that he'd snuck through when he first awoke, sending him past the room where he remembered hearing the blaring alarms. The room was now filled with people looking at monitors in silence. The device lit green and vibrated all over as he found that he was at the entrance of what Chloe had called the command center. The command group sat at the center of the room around a circular table with an opening at the middle, creating a ring where someone could walk inside. Inside the ring a person could stand on a platform to address the group. Joshua stepped into the domed room. They only occupied five seats out of the more than twenty available, which made the room feel larger.

Cade tapped on his handheld with a flat expression on his face, while Ian leaned back in a chair with his arms crossed and his leg lifted on the conference table.

"So, do we know what happened to the water?" Joshua asked.

Chloe shook her head. "The water just stopped flowing."

"The water lines run down toward the lower levels. Based on the information we have there should be a water-storage department. It has to be a part of the essential services and should be obvious once they find it and report back to us," Cade said.

"Wait, what do you mean by 'they'? Someone went back down?" Joshua interrupted.

"Well, how else do you expect us to get the water flowing again?" Cade looked offended.

"How many went down? Did they take any weapons? No one notified me!" Joshua stared at Ryan, who glanced away.

"Of course they took weapons. They need to defend themselves against any potential threats." Cade waved.

Joshua bit his lip. "You mean like any sents that might want to do harm?" Joshua asked.

Cade nodded. "Yes, sents or humans."

"You're still holding onto that one, are you?" Ian said.

"Yes. Someone must be controlling the technology behind this system. If it isn't us, then it must be someone else."

Joshua walked up to the table, pulling a chair out and rotating it to take a seat. "Okay. Let's take it one thing at a time. Any ideas about why we're out of water?

The door whooshed open behind Joshua. Ashley walked in with a woman he didn't recognize. Ashley had her arm wrapped around the other woman, helping to support her as she stepped in. "This is Meredith," Ashley said. "She recently woke up and wants to say something."

****

Meredith struggled to interpret truth from fallacy. There was a stark difference between what she was hearing from Ashley and what she remembered regarding how Legacy should have deployed itself. There was little to no overlap. Something very wrong had occurred here, but the chaos made it hard to know where to start. Legacy hadn't established a proper leadership as it should have. She also knew the development of a colonial establishment wouldn't occur until Legacy filled certain positions. Ashley had explained that there was no council, and with no official council in place, many steps needed to get taken to bring order and direction. Her muscles ached and pleaded with her to rest, even with the adrenaline she'd used earlier. It was working, but it quickly wore down her body. Her heart beat too fast. Her body was returning to a natural state, but she wouldn't be getting rest anytime soon. It was evident a lot needed to happen immediately.

There were no guiding rules or regulations established, and there appeared to be no clear chain of leadership or law enforcement. These things, and dozens more crucial oversights, bothered Meredith. A small tremor shook her hand as she reached for the table to sit down. One of the many side effects of memory transference. In time, it would pass.

"Thank you. I see no logged political or legal structure is established. Is this correct?"

She looked at the group one person at a time to read them individually, her intentional effort to establish leadership. Only one leaned back, indicating resistance. A man with bright white eyes. Almost oddly so.

She continued, "I can see from the state of Legacy and your lack of knowledge that something drastic has gone wrong. Can someone please provide me with a display unit?"

A reserved and shy man to her left shifted, then slid a device over. "Thank you, ah…" She paused, waiting for him to state his name.

"Ryan. My name is Ryan."

"Thank you, Ryan."

The display was familiar to her. With the tap of her fingertips and a few swipes, she was deep into the system. The database was intact, but only activated recently. Some systems reported an offline status, with a lack of water being the major priority to resolve. Full system checks revealed serious trouble. It was time for triage if anyone was going to survive. *Why did the system wait so long to wake me up?*

She checked the current user list to see who held presidential access and saw the role did not belong to anyone. She then checked for the representative of the people and again found an empty position. It was like that all the way down to mayor, but the mayoral seat had an event history. A user had had access at one point but lost it somehow. A user by the name of Richard.

"What happened to Richard?"

A man who was sitting stood. "Hello, I'm Joshua. Richard is recovering from some injuries." Injuries? She'd need to catalog that for further research.

"Before we all start assuming anything, let's not jump to the conclusion she was woken to take his place, because that's what it would be, an assumption," the man with bright white eyes said.

He was going to be a problem to deal with, and it took her a moment to decide on the best way to handle his accusation. She decided to take the naïve approach. She leaned back, unclasped her hands from the display, and spread her fingers to indicate an open and approachable stance.

"I have no desire to, nor did I express a desire to, take anyone's position. But I would like to suggest you take my unique perspective seriously."

"And what perspective is that?" the man snapped.

"Knowledge and understanding about things you are unaware of. I can answer many questions and help in establishing a working society. I'm not telling anyone what to do or even asking to take on any roles. I only wish to contribute to the best of my abilities. We are all in this together, and I only desire to be a positive member of the group."

The man leaned back slightly, staring for a moment but saying nothing.

"Don't pay any attention to Cade. Since he shot Michael, he's been banned from a lot of the critical areas and is unable to continue his work. Oh, and I'm Chloe." Chloe smiled.

"You shot someone?" Meredith asked, facing the man square on.

"I only stunned him. He was out of control. Michael had to be stopped. I don't see why the system felt I was the threat. I only did what was necessary at the moment."

"If you are correct and I gain the correct role, I will be happy to help restore your access after speaking with the department heads."

Cade shifted his head as if in thought. She answered the question that was unasked.

"The council will need to be established through a series of votes performed by the department heads. That is, the individuals who have been given leadership over the core departments of Legacy. Those roles have likely been filled, but no one knows it."

She tapped at the screen, pulling up the IDs of everyone in the room. "I see head of security is here." She nodded to Joshua. "As well as social work and administration." She glanced at Ashley before continuing.

"The council has two parts: the primary core group consisting of four individuals will be allowed to speak to I.R.I.S. on humanity's behalf. Once it's established, a secondary assembly is created consisting of a representatives to make the twelve. A full council is a group of twelve with I.R.I.S. making the odd vote. This is more practical in an active society. However, until the four are in place, the system will assume all power over us. It will continue to give and take roles as it deems fit."

The room fell silent. No one seemed to know how to deal with her.

"What are we going to do about the water?" Joshua asked.

"Oh, David should be reporting soon with their progress." Ryan walked to the entrance to tap on the display, presumably to check on David's status.

"So…David, and I hope others, went down with weapons to check on what exactly? How long have they been down there?" Joshua asked. "I was just in the shower and water stopped a few minutes ago."

"The water stopped flowing over an hour ago, but it took time for some of the local reserve tanks to run dry. The showers were attached to the reserve tanks because they were nonessential which also means this problem didn't just occur." Cade interjected.

Meredith picked up on Joshua mentioning weapons. Why would they need weapons? They were living in a closed-circuit environment. No in, and no out, until the planet was capable of sustaining life. Why would weapons have even been built? That was a waste of resources as well as a dangerous step toward destruction. Meredith made a mental note to research why Legacy had approved the building of weapons. That was certainly not an obvious choice a prime initiative with so many other forms of control available such as drugs and robotic enforcement. "What do they need protection from?"

Joshua said, "Sents that are killing people. We lost Nikolai, and now more lives are in danger."

"What did you expect? We had to do something. Without water, we'll only last a few days. We can't just sit around and wait," Cade said.

She delved deeper into the system through the handheld as they continued to discuss. Many types of robotic units had been built recently, but the system was not logging any of those currently connected. She read through the types, and one model jumped out as especially odd. Legacy had created a class of S-mBots. Why would military-grade Sentinels even be built? They would only be queued up by I.R.I.S. if the existence of the human race was threatened by outside forces or if humans were unable to manage themselves and were at risk of self-annihilation.

Neither case seemed to be in play here. She couldn't see any scenario that would end with sentinels harming people as Joshua was saying. That would defeat their purpose entirely. No, she needed to look into what was going on. To dig deeper to discover what had happened before they woke her. For instance, why would so many people have been birthed just to sleep for 25 years? Meredith found no signs of educational facilities with kids or the cities that provided living arrangements. Instead, they had military-grade quarters. They certainly didn't meet civilian standards.

A man on the opposite side of the group leaned back on his chair, shifting in pain. More of Michael's doing perhaps, or a sentinel's?

"You're right," She interjected. "Water is a vital part of survival and must get addressed. I do not understand why sentinels would have been issued kill orders, or by whom, but that can be dealt with in the programming. I think I can help out in that area, which should make this crisis manageable."

"Kill orders? The council? How is it that you know so much?" Cade asked.

"Because she had a successful mind map," Ashley replied.

The group looked at her for a long moment, processing what that meant.

"Do you know what happened to Legacy?" Chloe asked.

Meredith shook her head. "I'm sorry, but I don't. None of what is going on should have happened, and I will need some time to search through the system to figure out what's going on."

"How can you help with the sentinels?" Joshua asked.

She thought for a moment. "Well, someone would need to assume the role of mayor of the community. Once given that role, that individual would be able to establish the council by setting up the first vote, then we can begin to take ownership of the system and…"

"And here she shows how everything she said before about not wanting to take over was nothing but lies. Here she says that she's the best fit to be leader," Cade insisted.

Meredith didn't understand where all the hostility was coming from. Chloe stood abruptly and pointed a finger at Cade. "Cade. You're not helping. Meredith clearly understands how all this should be working. We should give her a shot. It's better than what we're doing now."

Meredith continued, "I need to talk to Richard. Give me some time to research, and after I meet with Richard, I will petition Legacy to allow me access to that role."

Heads were nodding in agreement. Cade threw up his hands in frustration, looking around at the group but saying nothing.

"Okay. Meredith will work on getting that done. But what are we going to do about the sents now?" Joshua asked.

"There might not be more of them. The others haven't seen any yet," Ryan said.

"How do you know that?" Cade asked

"Because I'm monitoring them. I've got someone back in my lab watching the feeds through their camera vests. If anything happens or they see anything, we'll get notified," Chloe said.

Chloe must be the head of information technologies. She had a firm grasp on the system. They'd have to talk later to discuss in more detail how much she'd learned. Hopefully, she'd be able to activate I.R.I.S., and things could return to normal.

"Well, I just can't sit here and wait. I'll get a gun and head down to help them," Joshua said.

"I'll go too," the injured man said with a grunt as he grabbed at his leg. He stood from his chair, using his hands to help him up.

"Ian, you can't go. You need to stay off that leg and rest." Joshua looked around, silently petitioning others to go, but no one offered to go with him.

He turned and left the room.

Chloe was next to leave, stating something about checking on the men who were canvassing the lower levels to follow the pipes. The rest followed her lead.

Ashley walked over and sat at the table next to Meredith. "Do you think you can help us?" Ashley asked.

Meredith thought about it. "I hope I can."

But she knew it would be a long journey.

Chapter 8
David

The lights mounted on David's vest were set at two opposing angles as he cautiously walked down the darkened tunnel. One lit his footsteps, and another, slightly to the left, shined on the curving hallway. He gripped the gun tightly and went through the process one more time. Cade had told him that he needed both hands firmly gripping the weapon for it to work—one hand around the trigger grip and the other up front to keep it level. By grabbing the handles firmly, David's hands would link him to the system, making the gun only fireable by him until someone else associated their credentials with the weapon. A small digital display identified him as User David-148. There was no way to know how powerful the gun was but he planned to unload on any sent he encountered. He didn't want to end up like Nikolai.

He shifted his weight, reacting to a noise. After a long pause, he questioned his sanity. He thought he heard a sound.

"Hello!" he called.

He didn't realize he had gone so far from the group. With too few people they were being spread thin to try to fix the water issue, and the lower levels were much larger than the top levels. David discovered a gradient cover that housed a series of pipes that lead him down a narrow alley and into yet another tunnel which stopped at a cave-in. He couldn't see how they'd repair everything. The rocks had done a considerable amount of damage to the pipe, stopping the water flow. At least that's what they were saying must have happened. In truth no one knew. Maybe he would be the one to resolve the problem.

He bent down, swinging the gun to his side and allowing the strap to hold it in place, then struggled to start moving the rocks out of the way. Another noise sounded. Quickly grabbing the gun, he shifted to see Ethan standing in front of him. Ethan turned his hands up, his gun dropping to the floor. The sound echoed through the tunnel.

"Stop! It's me!" he said.

"What are you doing here? I thought you were investigating that other tunnel." He turned back to the stones and continued pulling rocks away.

"There was a bunch of rubble that fell like this, so I turned back around to find another way. What are you doing?" Ethan asked.

"I'm trying to get through. I think the pipe running down this tunnel could be the main water line. The rocks could have crushed the pipe, stopping the water flow. We need to clear a path. Come help me."

Ethan turned back, looking into the darkness. His vest lit the floor and shined into the long tunnel. He hesitated before turning back around.

"Oh, okay. I'll help you since I have nothing better to do," he said.

David pretended not to notice the color that had drained from his face. He began to pull at the stone. After a few minutes, Ethan took a couple of steps back, then walked up and over the fallen rock.

"This is going to take forever. Step back." Ethan pulled his gun up and pointed at a boulder blocking the path.

"Wait, what if we make things worse?"

Ethan tilted his head in thought. "You're right." He then stepped back a few more feet. "The surrounding area is stable enough. It's just this area that was weak. We should be okay."

Ethan began to play with his gun. David hastily stepped aside, unsure how much he could trust Ethan not to shoot either of them.

"Here we go," Ethan said.

A loud humming sound started as the gun shot a bright light. A small object or maybe an energy pulse pushed out so fast he barely realized what had happened. The electricity forked through the air, penetrating into the rubble. The light bounced off one of the larger rocks and blinded them for a few moments, but otherwise made little to no change to their progress.

David looked down at Ethan's gun, then at his own. They had some similarities and differences. Each had a short stock and a long barrel that reached out two feet forward behind the body, but David's had a larger secondary barrel. On the side of his gun, a display offered a series of options with a corresponding severity-level adjustment. After filtering through them, David reached a feature called Controlled Demolition. With the option selected and set for level six of ten, David shot at the center of a large rock. The gun let loose a series of pulsating synchronized lights and gave a firm kick against his shoulder. The pulses were followed by a blast of energy, creating a shockwave that threw Ethan off his feet. Dust filled the area, preventing them from seeing anything. Rocks bounced off the walls and rolled to his feet. Once the dust settled, he saw the larger stones were broken into smaller pieces.

"I think there are basically more rocks now? Not sure how much help it was," David said.

"The big rocks are smaller," Ethan replied. "That's a good thing."

David didn't mention that more rocks had fallen from the broken level above them. *So much for controlled demolition.*

The vest lights moved with their motions over the stones. David helped Ethan up, and they started to evaluate the progress they'd just made. It really was hard to tell if they had achieved any. Heat could be felt a few feet back from where he stood.

Ethan stepped up and reached out to touch some debris, but pulled back when he got closer. "The stone is hot!"

Something caught David's eye. He stepped closer and peered into the rocks. "What's that?" He stared at something that wasn't a rock, but had the familiar shape of fingers. It was a hand. He struggled to his feet, shaking his head.

"My ears are ringing!" Ethan screamed.

"Quiet!"

"What?" Ethan yelled, trying to clean his ears with his fingers to stop the ringing. "I can't hear anything you're saying!"

He placed his hand over Ethan's mouth then pointed.

Ethan pulled David's hand away. "That's a hand?" Still too loudly.

David slapped him on the back of his head. "Of course, now hold on for a second."

David stepped closer, bent down, and blew the dust away. Their lights bounced off the metal surface of the hand. Ethan edged closer to him. Just as David reached out to touch the hand, a voice came from behind them.

"Hey, get over here!" a guy said, startling them out of their trance. They looked at each other and laughed nervously. Without a word spoken David decided to let it go but made a mental note that there were dangers around every corner. That robot could have been alive. They'd need to be more careful.

"We found something," the man said. David couldn't remember his name.

"We'll come back," David said.

They nodded in agreement then followed the man into a huge open tunnel. The base was broad, almost thirty feet wide, and it was twenty feet tall at the highest point. A group of guys knelt, huddled around something on the floor.

David drew near, then froze when he recognized that it was a sent, different from the remains of what Chloe had destroyed. This one was mostly intact, but without a head.

David and Ethan pushed their way through the group.

"What happened here?" Ethan asked.

The question went unanswered. One of the guys knelt to inspect further.

"Where's the head?" David asked.

After a preliminary search produced nothing, they returned to the body. The sent's limbs were sprawled as if it had crawled there. Its body was severely damaged, with wires pulled out on the floor.

One guy said, "It crawled from this door."

David turned and discovered a liquid trail that leaked from the sent and led to a doorway. David walked to the door and placed his hand on the sphere, but nothing happened.

"Oh, I know what needs to happen," a shorter guy with black hair said. The guy took the sphere from the wall and sat on the floor, cutting and merging wires together. After a few minutes, he stood.

"The power line is connected but there's nothing getting to the panel. Let me see if I can override the fuse." He looked around, then identified a panel farther down the hallway. He explained more about how the power worked as he opened the panel and reached in elbows deep. His muffled voice could barely be heard from inside the wall. "Yeah, that might work." Some banging and a curse, then, "Okay, I think it'll open now."

David pressed again, and the sphere lit. Ethan stepped up to the door with his gun pointed at the center crack.

"Open it," he said.

When he pressed the sphere like he would the ones from the upper level, the door swished open. Ethan leaped back and fired his gun, which released a stream of blinding light and deafening sound. David stared at him once the gun stopped shooting, stunned. Ethan's eyes were closed, his finger still on the trigger. The gun had been depleted of all its energy.

"Ethan, we're good. Open your eyes."

Nothing was coming out of the room or moving. Whatever Ethan had seen, it was surely dead or stunned. He took a cautious step into the room, everyone else waiting behind to see what was going to happen next. The gun was ready to fire at the slightest sound. After a moment his eyes began to acclimate to the darkness once more. He saw something metallic and froze. Ethan stepped up behind him and shined his lights ahead.

The forms before them were unmistakably horrid. They were sents in different positions. Two were frozen at the door's opening. One was down on the ground as if it was trying to crawl to the doorway, while two others were beaten up and in pieces on the floor.

Ethan bent down to one of the sents, reached out, and knocked twice on its head. "I destroyed it," Ethan said, smiling.

David shook his head. "Your gun didn't do any damage." David pointed to the sent. "Look, there are no markings. Just dents where someone beat it."

One of the guys pointed to the ceiling. "Those marks up there." He indicated the rim of the door frame. "Those are you."

The group had come to the door, the sent without a head forgotten. They were peering inside the room.

"I had to have hit one. I was only two feet away. There's no way I missed," Ethan said.

David ducked and skirted his way around the sents to get into the room. It was square, with some chairs along the back wall. Possibly a meeting room. Some chairs along the back wall were scattered about the floor on their backs and sides, likely thrown around in whatever battle had occurred here. Ethan stayed behind him, followed by a few more of the guys. After scanning the room, he saw another door on the opposite side from the entrance. The sphere was lit.

David walked to it and pressed down with his right hand. The display above read: *Access Denied*, then went back to a scrolling marquee asking him to press his hand on the sphere. After pressing again and getting the same result, David decided to move on and investigate the rest of the room.

The door shut, cutting them off from the remainder of the group.

Ethan whimpered nearby, and David was about to say something when he realized that this side didn't have a sphere. There was no way to open the door from the inside. That was strange.

Ethan banged his fists against the steel barrier. "Open up!"

The door slid open.

"Wow, is this door voice activated?"

"No, I opened it," said the guy who originally fixed the door. He had apparently pressed the sphere.

"Someone needs to stay near the door to keep it open," Ethan demanded weakly.

Just as the lights from the other men flashed through the open door, David noticed a smaller sent. It couldn't have been much more than five feet, with thin arms and legs. Nothing like the others. They appeared to have been built for heavy duty tasks while he couldn't guess what this one's purpose would be.

"Shine your light over here." David pointed to the sent. It looked just like a naked woman. The group started to move, their lights shimmering off the female sent's skin.

What would a sent like this be doing here? Something dimly blinked on its neck. David leaned in to get a better look. It pulsed with a bright white light and turned blue, then a series of lights flashed through its body. In an instant and before they could raise their guns, the sent lifted its hands.

"Please, do not destroy me. I mean you no harm. I am low on power." A pause. It lowered its head. "Charge me." It returned to its original position before it almost silently pleaded, "Help me."

It lay down in the corner of the room and curled up in the fetal position, looking down at the floor. Its lights blinked one last time before turning off.

"We should destroy it!" one man said.

No one disagreed, but David wondered why this one was so different. Why it had acted that way. Why hadn't it taken advantage of the situation and tried to kill them like the other sent had done?

"No. It shut down. I think it ran out of power." David pointed his gun away from the sent to show he felt safe. He hoped the rest would follow his lead. They did. Then David had a thought. "We should take it up to Chloe. I bet she can find out why this particular sent is so different."

"Why this one?" one of the guys asked.

"Do you think you can carry one of those?" David pointed to the sent near the entrance. "The bigger one is probably around nine feet tall if you put all the pieces together. Plus this is the one that asked for our help. This is the one that spoke to us rather than attacked us."

The guy looked at the larger robots, then to the smaller one. "Okay, let's take this one."

Chapter 9
Joshua

"Chloe, where are they now?" Joshua asked over his vest comm unit.

A slight pause. "They're on level four."

Joshua climbed down, crossing the third access panel. The gun hung from his left shoulder. The vest lights showed his way down. All the gear was surprisingly easy to carry. The vest was sleek and formfitting. When turned on, it conformed to the shape of his body, almost blending into the uniform and creating a second, thicker layer of clothing. He was carrying three more vests to act as repeaters in case he ran into places with no power at all.

"They're following a large pipe from three," Chloe said.

Her voice reverberated out of his vest and bounced against the walls of the tight access shaft. Once on the fourth level, Joshua redirected his lights forward and down. The display over his right eye identified anything recognizable. Gun at his side, he started sweeping the immediate area. The access panel opened to a curving hallway. He left one vest to repeat the signal from above so he could stay connected. Once he knew he was safe, Joshua scanned the handheld to check for the group. The eerie silence divided the occasional creak and ping that echoed in the distance. The handheld showed the group moving toward him. He tapped his screen, and a dozen names popped up. David was separate from the group, but Ethan was with them. He tapped on Ethan's name.

"Ethan. I'm down here and coming to you."

He was surprised that Ethan had chosen to help. Joshua remembered pulling Ethan up after Michael pushed him down days earlier. *You never know who will step up when the moment calls for it*, Joshua thought.

After a long silent moment, Ethan's voice came over his comm unit. "We can use the help. This place is huge and pipes are running in all kinds of directions."

"Okay, I'm headed your way now."

Joshua turned left and started following the blips on his handheld. Noticing that his gun had a clip on top that allowed for the display to connect, he attached it and started moving toward the group. This configuration allowed him to glance up at his screen, yet still keep both hands on the gun.

As he walked toward the group he realized they were curving away from him. They must be on a different set of hallways, because his path wouldn't intersect theirs. He decided to check a few rooms to find if there was a way to cross over. After a dozen locked doors, none of which had power, he realized most rooms would be off-limits. Each one remained locked until he found one set of doors blown off their frame.

On the opposite side of the hallway, the door protruded out of the curved wall. Joshua stepped over broken pieces of another door and placed another vest down to ensure connectivity. Once through, he looked for signs of danger. Seeing no sents or potential cave-ins, he checked the handheld. Its telemetry data displayed the map of the surrounding environment using its built-in sensors. The room measured one hundred feet tall and at least that much in width and length. At first, he didn't understand how such a large room could exist, and then he realized that the upper levels had been built around the room. That explained the hallways with no rooms. They had been built around structures like this one. Joshua squinted into the abyss. In the distance, he saw multiple levels of walkways halfway up with rooms that looked similar to what they'd awoken in.

The lights from his vest could only shine so far with nothing for them to contact. Their beams dissolved into the deep darkness. He started to move across the room to the other side, where he thought he would be able to intersect with the group. He was unconsciously walking to his right to find the perimeter. The darkness called out to him, as though it watched his every step. He felt like it wanted to know what he was doing, why he was intruding. Without realizing it, he found his hands gripping his weapon tightly.

He knew what was keeping him on edge. He couldn't see any walls, only darkness in every direction. The doorway was gone. His heart began to beat faster. The quiet, unsettling stillness of walking in the darkness was getting to him. The handheld provided some reassurance. The screen told him that the walls were there. One was not too far from him.

Walking toward it as if the device were lying to him, he paused when he recognized dividers protruding out. In each one sat something he'd hoped never to see again. He stopped and held his breath, trying not to make a sound. He remembered Nikolai's body being dragged.

There were thirty, maybe forty sents, lined up in rows. Fear filled his belly and rose up within him. Heat flushed his face. After an eternal moment, he breathed out in an attempt to relax. The action pushed his mind into movement. Every one of them was powered down. He relaxed some as he stepped closer. They were different in design from the one that had tried to kill them, and which Chloe had ultimately destroyed. The sents triggered something vague within him. A notion in his mind. He closed his eyes and tried to concentrate on it. Lately, he found if he focused on the feeling, it brought the memory to the surface.

Joshua worked hard to forget about the sents around him. After a few deep breaths, a flash came to him. He remembered being in this room. On the other side, though. Joshua opened his eyes and started walking to the spot where the vague memory that was rising to the surface of his mind drew him. He could see it now. Sents were waiting for activation. They were sents waiting to assist in training. Something was slowly coming back to him. He looked across the vastness to see an opening splitting the row of sents.

The moment Joshua saw the door, his mind flashed. He paused once more and concentrated. Committing his focus to remembering. To being in that memory and ignore his current surroundings.

Before he knew it he remembered walking through the room. But it was fully powered, with people and sentinels busy performing exercises in what he now knew to be a training facility. He was coming to check on a friend. A half dozen guards stood at the entrance. He stepped up and offered his identification. They all knew him, but it was the procedure.

Inside he walked up to a sent that was painted in red and white with a green cross over its chest.

"Where is Galen?"

The sent pointed to a bed in the opposite corner. Just as Joshua started to go, he overheard the soldiers talking.

"They've found one of them," one of the soldiers said.

"One of the rebels is getting interrogated."

The smell of blood permeated the air. Blood and sweat. He walked along the wall, which turned into a narrow hallway. He had an urgent feeling. A need to be somewhere. To be inside. This was not a casual visit, but a mission. Joshua felt the strong impression that he was going somewhere, and if he was caught, his trip would lead to a permanent death. He needed to know if they existed. People talked of rebels and the illegal sentinels, but he'd never taken them seriously.

He found the interrogation room and rushed over to a nearby observational chamber to turn the comms on. He opened a channel so the video feed would stream to his handheld. He didn't recognize the man sitting on the chair. The uniform reflected that he belonged to the mechanical division. The sent interviewing the man was pacing back and forth angrily. Behavior he'd never seen sentinels display. It walked to a nearby table and yanked a cover off a cart. Black sentinel parts lay in a series of containers on the cart. Joshua could see scratches on them. It must have gone through a severe beating before it was ripped apart like that.

He zoomed in. The torso sat on the table over the smaller pieces. The sentinel punched the man in the face, sending him and the chair to the floor. Blood shot out of the man's mouth and sprayed onto the wall behind them. Joshua had to find out what was going on. Using his handheld, he turned on the volume so he could hear the conversation.

A tall, skinny sentinel that had remained silently still to that point stood and walked over to the pieces on the table. It touched the chest and passed its fingers over the scratches. "Have you seen this unit before?"

Another sentinel picked up the now-weeping man. He shook his head.

"No, I have never seen it. It was in the pipes when I went down there. It leaped out and started dragging me into the hole. That's when the other sentinel—" he nodded to the sentinel that had just hit him, "—saved me and attacked that thing." The man jerked his chin to the broken parts.

There was an awkward pause during which the sentinels froze in place. The blood was freely flowing from the man's mouth. Then the door slid open. The sentinels exited the room, pushing the cart with the metal pieces.

Joshua waited until he thought the hallway would be clear and opened the door. He made his way back to the infirmary and found Galen.

A sentinel inspected a metallic arm as his friend screamed, "Come on. Be quick about it! I don't have all day. I can't take the pain!"

Another sentinel attempted to attach a leg to him, but he was moving too much. His arm had tubes connected, indicating the distribution of painkillers. A stray thought about addiction to the medications popped into his head. It was a common habit for the lower-level citizens. Joshua had a distinct memory of this guy's body requiring much more than the average dosage. The first sentinel walked over and pressed Galen's waist down onto the table, allowing the leg to be attached. Joshua could see tiny objects moving on his leg and connecting to the body. A translucent material appeared around the seam, blending the skin and the metal perfectly. After a moment he spun around and stood on the leg as if it were a part of his body. He jumped a few times before seeing Joshua.

"Hey, Josh. How's it going, man?"

Galen wobbled, almost falling. A sent caught him and pulled him up, guiding him back to the bed. It asked if he'd rather lie down.

"The idiot got caught halfway in the turbine down in the manufacturing plant. He's lucky it didn't split him clear in two."

The voice was familiar. It sounded like someone important to him but he couldn't place it. It rang from behind, but when Joshua turned to see who it was, he was back in the training room. Alone and in the darkness.

Joshua stepped up to the doors and pressed against them. Nothing happened, and nothing would happen until they had power running to them. He made his way through the room and to the other side to find another locked door. The handheld on his gun showed the group was walking along a hallway that would pass directly on the other side of the door.

He started to shout when the screen showed they were just feet away. "Hey, hold up! I'm right here!"

He looked down and noticed that they'd stopped. He heard a muffled voice from the other side. "Joshua! Is that you?"

"Yes, I'm here. I can't get through."

"Hold on for a moment. We're trying to get the door opened."

Joshua remembered how difficult it would be to pry it open, then thought of the doors on the other side, and the ones that were in pieces and shot into the opposite wall of the hallway. What could have done so much damage? Another one of the bombs perhaps? Or maybe some directional explosives? There was no way to get the doors open manually.

Just as he started to search for another way around, the door slid open. A man leaned out from the sphere on the other side. Apparently he was able to open doors that weren't powered. That could be useful.

"Thanks." Joshua extended his hand to him.

"No problem. I'm Zhang," the short man said, shaking his hand.

A few of the guys had a sent in their arms. It was small and somewhat feminine, which was strange. In many ways this one was different from all the others, but that was a distraction. They needed to focus on the real issue at hand.

"What's going on? Have you found the issue with the water?" he asked, staring at the sent.

"We're bringing this up to Chloe so she can take a look at it."

That made sense. Chloe had already studied the other sent. He turned to Zhang. "Can you work on getting power to this entire area?"

Zhang looked into the room and nodded. "I think so. I've been working on the primary power line that feeds into all the lower levels. We made it past levels two and three, so it will not take much to also get the power working on this level. I'm going to need to go through all the wiring to find the fault points. I'll get to work on that now."

Joshua wasn't sure exactly what Zhang was talking about, but he nodded. The two other men continued with the sent.

Joshua turned to Ethan. "What's David doing?"

"He's following the water pipes," Ethan said.

"Okay, let's go meet him while they bring the sent up to Chloe."

Joshua turned to the two guys carrying the sent. "Once you're done, come back down and help Zhang finish restoring power to this level. We need to know the purpose of this place. It's important."

Zhang started to walk toward a nearby panel.

"And Zhang?"

He paused. Joshua pointed toward the infirmary that he remembered.

"Start with getting that room over there up and running. The one in the middle. Okay?"

Zhang looked, nodded, then started walking in the direction Joshua had pointed.

Chapter 10
Chloe

A three-dimensional image of a spacecraft hovered two feet above the holographic display Cade had turned on. A planet labeled *Earth* grew smaller and smaller the greater the distance grew from its home. Chloe wasn't sure what information she'd learn from the program, but with the description explaining the projected path and installation of Legacy, how could she not be intrigued?

She sat intently, watching the ship curve around planets, stars, and asteroids, leaving a solar system. A ticking clock sped up above the surface of the desk in front of her. She stood and walked around the hologram, getting the full view.

"Apparently the ship originated on a planet called Earth. For some reason, all data collected for this installation has been erased or is not available to us at this time. This is merely a generic example and not an explanation of how our particular installation occurred," Cade said.

Being in the same room with Cade was difficult enough, but having the memory of them kissing haunted her mind. Chloe kept thinking of the dream and how they'd embraced, as well as her feelings for him at the moment. She couldn't deal with the idea of ever having feelings like that for him.

Cade remained focused on the system, intent on narrating the process. "See here. This is where the planet is discovered. This would represent where we are now."

She watched the ship reach a planet. Data from various scans appeared, showing viability factors. Small objects shot out of the ship, landed on the surface, and started gathering samples. The hologram highlighted each transitional point in the process. Chloe was having trouble keeping track of how much time had elapsed. The clock indicated days, or cycles, around the nearby star. After sixty cycles of the planet around the sun, the ship ejected an object. The hologram changed, zooming in on the object. The speed increased, and the target on the surface was illuminated while the fall turned into a controlled spiral pattern. Without slowing down, the object shot deep beneath the surface of the planet and stopped just short of a deposit of something highlighted. It was a large deposit of iron.

"Here, I can change the video depending on the type of planet Legacy encounters," Cade interjected.

"So, if what we are living in is not what was meant to happen, what is an installation of Legacy supposed to be like?" Chloe asked.

"Good question. This is no more than a projected plan of the standard setup, likely made back on Earth." Cade pointed to a set of large deposits of what the system labeled *Ideal Composite Minerals.* An oval object started to break up the surrounding ore. "I chose this example to indicate a similar installation. The large mass the device is beginning to work on is mostly iron. The device appears to be the milling-factory version that allows it to take the base minerals to develop tools."

Cade zoomed in where the unit was releasing small sents. They attached themselves to drills and began to mine the iron. He moved forward through the video, skipping thirty more cycles until a building appeared, and the smaller sents disappeared as they were consumed by the equipment to be replaced with larger, more capable sents. The whole process took a few hundred cycles of the planet, but the final result was a functional structure.

"That is the process Legacy goes through, no matter which installation I select. Even if the planet is habitable, the initial installation is underground, which makes harvesting minerals easier. It just builds up to the surface rather than down like this installation. There are many different types of installations, from full colonies to fueling stations and research facilities. The result is a shielded enclosure for humans to protect us from any danger."

The sents began working on the surrounding mineral deposits, connecting structures together with tunnels. More work was done, followed by more cycles passing. The moving parts produced a factory deep below the surface, and through that creation, larger human-sized sents developed. These sents accelerated the work on Legacy.

"The odd thing is—" Cade began to flip through the options, "—each option was revealing a different facility depending on what the planet required. None of these setups fit our structure. Parts of each example can be seen throughout Legacy."

Cade flipped to one setup.

"This one involves terraforming a planet that needs more oxygen but only requires a refinery, a terraforming plant, and something called a control tower to manage the sents."

The video changed drastically into a larger facility that involved structures on the surface.

"This one is a setup for military purposes. This version is if Legacy encounters hostile forces. What we are finding is that this more accurately reflects our design. The latest scans from the group down at the third level suggest hostile deployment more than any of the other options, but other areas fit the research stations. A few levels down there are five different kinds of research stations interconnected," Cade said.

Chloe couldn't deny his hypothesis. The presence of the guns alone supported the idea. However, if Legacy had developed itself to counter hostile forces, then where were those forces now? And why did it look like whatever battle was fought, nobody won?

"The strange thing is what happens when I try to access Legacy's current floor plans." Cade pulled up a query request for the plans. "See?"

Chloe looked closely at the screen. "No plans are available?" she asked.

"No data was collected while we slept. All we have is from what we have discovered using the vests and handhelds at this moment."

"So, Legacy decided to install every variation at one place? Something must be wrong with its programming." Chloe reached out to the image. Sents worked with each other throughout the facility, going about their tasks. A large pipe led to the surface, allowing for the venting of chemicals into the atmosphere.

"Chloe, are you there?" came a voice from a nearby panel.

Chloe looked up and around, attempting to get a sense of the direction of the sound. She randomly chose to the right.

"Uh, yeah. I'm here. Is that you, Ryan?"

"It's me. I was able to get the intercom system working through most areas where power is restored. If I could only find a better way to locate people. I tried five different rooms before I found you. At first, I thought it would be easy with how the system labels the handhelds to match the person using them, but when I pulled your ID up, it said that you were here with me. Of course, you weren't here. You were there, or wherever you were at the time. It was just your handheld. Then I—"

"What do you need, Ryan?" Chloe asked.

A long silence. "I've been digging into the data from Legacy, and I found a video that explains a lot. You wanted to know about the beds and how they worked? Which node are you on?"

It surprised Chloe how quickly Ryan was learning the system. She often felt that she knew so much about Legacy because of the memories she had, but she was the only one. Ryan just seemed to figure it out without trying very hard. She pressed the ID button at the bottom right of the screen, which gave her various pieces of information, including the node ID of the unit. Node IDs made tracking and communication possible. Without specific node numbers, broadcast channels would be the only way to send any communication, making it impossible to have something as complex as Legacy.

"I'm at 2.134.3," Chloe answered.

"Okay. Level two, room one-thirty-four, and display three. I got it. I'll send it over now."

A request to accept an incoming message displayed at the bottom center of the screen. Chloe tapped on it, and the video started playing. It showed a bed similar to the ones that they slept on. Chloe had stopped using hers days ago. She couldn't seem to get any rest on it, even with the tubes giving her whatever they were giving her.

"This video shows the purpose of the beds and how we got here. It's called *In Vitro Fertilization*."

The video replaced her current screen with an image of a bed. Through pipes, it received the required substances to birth a human. Some sperm and an egg were flushed into a sack, floating in the liquid. The same liquid that they'd all woken up drenched in. Chloe still shuddered when thinking about how it was all over her body.

The sack went through the stages of life. A fetus started growing, and through time, transitioned into a child. At varying stages, the fluid would drain while arms performed surgery and attached the injection points for the tubes. The infant grew inside its artificial womb.

"I was performing an inventory of all beds with people living in them and one was added today," Ryan said.

Another request for display control came up, and Chloe tapped the *Accept* button. Ryan flipped through the software, bringing up a life-inventory category which listed more than a hundred people. Some were lit green, some yellow, and others bold, flashing red. The green life forms represented the people who were awake. The yellow were people still sleeping, and red were the people who had died when the water ran out.

Ryan pointed at the profiles in red, "They died in their sleep." His face was flush as he frowned.

Chloe new people were beginning to panic and she knew another riot would break out once they learn people have died. Chloe thought about all the people still sleeping. Why hadn't they woken? Why did some wake up while others remained asleep? She almost missed the name as she scanned through the sleepers: Nikolai.

"Is that Nikolai? Why does it say that he's sleeping?"

"Right. I went to Nikolai's room. It's sealed shut. The bed has the glass enclosure filled with the liquid. Check this out."

The monitor highlighted Nikolai's name, and his bed was brought up. The age next to it was four hours and twenty-five minutes. This information couldn't be correct. Nikolai was dead.

"That must be wrong. Why would it say that Nikolai is four hours old? His body is down the hallway."

"But look at the number behind his name: 149."

Four-hour-old Nikolai was not the Nikolai they knew. He was the beginning of a new life. "We were born in the beds?" The thought sent a shiver down Chloe's spine.

The door opened, letting in the sound of metal dragging on the floor. "Chloe, we have something you need to look at," one of the men who'd gone to fix the water said.

She looked intently at the screen and could barely make out something covered with a large cloth in the background.

Ryan was looking off screen. "Over there. Yeah, take all that off the table. Chloe. You'll want to come back to your lab." Ryan sounded curious.

"What's wrong?"

"You'll need to see this for yourself."

Chapter 11
Meredith

"To start," Meredith repeated, "we'll need to establish the council."

They were walking through the commissary, where people were eating and talking. Except for the neutral uniforms, it could have been a standard military base back on Earth.

"What is the council's purpose?" Ashley asked.

"Well, the chaotic manner in which Legacy is operating currently is because I.R.I.S. isn't responding. I.R.I.S. should be assisting us as we struggle to find out what's going on. Legacy is not designed to manage humans. It is more of a data-management system for I.R.I.S. Even though it does contain some built-in intelligence, these functions are highly restricted to the particular purposes for which they were created. The A.I. is smart enough to protect itself and ensure it will continue, but has no value system for humanity. As far as it's concerned, we are no different from the benches we sit on or the doors we walk though. We are tools to be used."

It took Meredith by surprise, how much she knew about Legacy. Something inside of her remained calm about it all. She remembered being on Earth and giving her life for Legacy. She remembered being in the chair and Dr. Katherine Witaford herself reassuring her a new life would be waiting for her when she woke, how it would seem no more than a dream and she would be one of the thousands of people continuing human life on a far-off planet. She'd wake up in her bed, in her new home, and in a younger, genetically superior body free of disease. She would start over with the benefit of wisdom beyond her years, disease free.

That was what had gotten her to leave everything behind. It hadn't been hard when she was leaving a death sentence from an incurable disease. At no point had all this been a part of the plan. They had said the unpredictability of nature would likely force Legacy and I.R.I.S. to adapt in obscure and strange ways, but they hadn't prepared her for this scenario. She needed a holo-lens, or at least a handheld connected to I.R.I.S., to start learning what kind of structure had been built and what had led to the destruction. Why would I.R.I.S. grow human life in such an unstable structure rather than spend its energy creating the proper sentinels to assist in any challenges it faced? The question didn't bring much comfort. This certainly wasn't the Legacy she'd dreamed about.

"How do we turn I.R.I.S. on?" Ashley asked, pulling Meredith out of her thoughts.

"Well, I need to learn a great deal, but first things first. We need to call for a vote. Once the council is established, we can start making decisions. Legacy will operate under the rule of the council."

"Okay, how does that work?"

They made their way into a nearby tunnel heading toward…she wasn't sure. She felt like walking. Her legs were a little weak, but she understood she needed to push them to help the circulation. The bed hadn't done a perfect job in avoiding atrophy. Her muscles felt weak. Either they needed to grow, or the planet's gravity was different from Earth's. Probably stronger. Maybe it was larger.

"We must initialize the software within the core system and give people a chance to put forward their names to be voted upon."

"That sounds easy enough."

"It should be. Especially if we can get only one name per position for voting. A debate and vote will occur if more than one person runs. Otherwise, it's an automatic process and will be challenged at the next cycle of elections. A vote must occur before Legacy gives us more power. We must prove we are capable of managing ourselves."

A man stepped out through the crowd. "And I presume you're aspiring to be the president?"

Meredith paused as she glanced toward the voice. Her mouth gaped slightly at the sight of the man walking towards her. She remembered seeing him in training. She worked hard to remember the many names and skill sets of people involved in the project. What was his name? His skill set was political, but she couldn't remember his specialty. It came to her as she reached to shake his hand. Edward Watkins.

"Edward, is it?"

His face showed surprise. "Edward. Yes. How did you know? I am Edward-148."

She tried to avoid the question by changing the subject. "I only aspire to serve."

His eyes rolled just for a second then he smiled. "That sounds like a great attitude. I admire that in an individual. I plan to enter my name to be considered to replace Richard if I can only find out how to do so. The manuals are lengthy and filled with thousands of documents from law to philosophy, but we've recently made some progress."

Edward-148? What did that mean? Had Legacy grown variations of him at this point? She couldn't imagine any situations requiring this many attempts to grow the same human. The idea of such actions occurring was upsetting. What was triggering the repetition? And if Legacy had produced a hundred and forty-eight Edwards, what had happened to them? Had they all died? The odds of that seemed unlikely.

She tried to find the logic behind it all. Behind everything. But without I.R.I.S.'s connection to Legacy many things would be much more challenging. Something could have destroyed I.R.I.S. If that was the case, she didn't see a way to save them. I.R.I.S. alone had the knowledge of what humans had accomplished on Earth. She wondered how long ago that had been. If Edward was the 148th, and each of him had lived healthy, long lives—which was possible—then theoretically Legacy had been on this planet for thousands of years.

"There are four positions to be voted on first, and the system selects the fifth. The four powers are the heads of the four states of government, and the fifth makes the deciding vote in case of ties."

"I was able to read about the four states of government: the president who represents the people, the representative of material and distribution, the representative of technology, and the philosopher to express the mind of the people. I did not fully understand the purpose of the fifth other than to deal with ties."

"The fifth is most important. It is the individual whom I.R.I.S. decides is most capable of seeing life as truthfully as possible. It is often the wisest and most reliable. Usually, the fifth operates under the direct guidance and guardianship of I.R.I.S. Raised by her, that individual takes on the mind of I.R.I.S. to speak on her behalf."

"You talk like I.R.I.S. is a person."

"She is often viewed as such, with more of a capacity to be a sentient being than any of us have. She was more of everything than we will ever hope to have: a longer existence, more knowledge and experience, as well as the ability to process an exorbitant amount of data to provide the best decision possible. But she is only one voice, and her proxy represents one vote. She can only exert some degree of power. It is up to the others to utilize her knowledge and advice to the best of humanity's ability."

"Personally," Edward said, "I am considering the role of president. We need a level-headed person. Not like Richard. A lot of the issues we are dealing with are directly related to him. Situations like Michael. We can't let him sit in a cell or let him go free."

Michael's name continued to be mentioned. He must have caused some issues. They said he had beaten Richard.

Ashley stepped between Meredith and Edward. "So what are you talking about? If he can't be locked up or set free, then what other options are you considering?"

Ashley stared at Edward, waiting for him to speak. Then Cade showed up.

"Am I interrupting?"

Meredith was happy for the distraction. With so many things happening at once, she needed time to process before she could start acting mindfully, knowing she was taking the most appropriate steps.

She needed to gather more information and talk with people like Michael and Richard.

"No, not at all," she said.

"Well, then," he said, looking to Ashley—her face still red with anger—then to Edward and finally back to Meredith. "I thought you might want one of these."

Cade handed her a handheld device before continuing, "I've modified the permissions you'll need to access Legacy and remain in sync with all of our devices. If you need to communicate with any of us, all you have to do is select the name."

Meredith was caught off guard by his gesture. He had previously come off as being a hard person, someone who didn't do this kind of thing. In her experience, people like him always had a motive other than being helpful. There must have been a reason for this. Maybe just to try to get on her good side, but somehow she didn't think so. Ashley was still staring at Edward in heated silence with arms crossed.

"Thank you, Cade. I appreciate it."

"No problem at all. Also, Chloe is working on a sent that was brought up. I thought you'd like to know." He pointed to the screen. "Click this button, you'll get the live video feed."

Cade clicked it, and she watched as Chloe moved a metal arm. Multiple angles were being shown from different points in the room. It looked like the cameras were on people walking around wearing militaristic vests.

"That's a sent?"

"Very lifelike. Don't you think?"

This was beyond strange. There had never been any intention of building sentinels this similar to humans.

All sentinels were purposefully designed to be bipedal to be effective, but different enough to create the psychological distance humans needed to feel comfortable. It was well established that people had a difficult time fearing sentinels when they looked like them. There is a natural tendency to separate from that which is different. Earth's governments had learned that early on. People had trouble getting used to humanoid sentinels. She was certain that there had never been code introduced to I.R.I.S. to design sentinels this similar to people. How had this one been built?

"She does look human," she said. "Except for the obvious outer metal layer. But the movement of her body…I wouldn't be able to tell the difference."

Her mind trailed off in thought about the implications of I.R.I.S. building a sentinel that seemed so human, creating a new model of sentinel.

"I say we shoot him. He's proving to be too dangerous, and at this point, he's a drain on our resources," Edward said, ignoring the conversation with Cade.

An awkward silence drew out, with Cade looking between them all trying to figure out what they were talking about. Ashley looked to be in pure shock, but Edward continued before she said anything.

"And what would you do with Michael?" He asked, directing the question to Meredith.

She thought for a moment before speaking. "I wouldn't kill the man. I, as of right now, do not have enough information to advise you about the situation adequately."

"This is why we need someone like me." Edward began to speak louder so the surrounding people could hear. "If we work together we can figure out how to perform the repairs. We can accomplish anything. We do not need another leader who has no clue what's going on."

He correctly thought Meredith wanted to become president and would use anything he could to gain an advantage. She would have to be careful about how she communicated from now on. Everyone would be watching and monitoring.

A man walked up to Edward, and they started to whisper together. Edward placed his palm on a handheld device. Meredith recognized the software he was using. He turned to address the crowd with the device held up high.

She understood what was going on. Edward had just submitted his identity to be president. She didn't want to necessitate an election, but she had to admit, she was the most appropriate person. Meredith knew how things should be and could pull from her years of training on Earth. It was all there in her head, but she needed to gain the right privileges to use it which meant she needed the position of president to make the greatest impact. If Edward claimed the position, he'd have to approve everything. No, she would have to do the same to initiate the vote, or the system would automatically make him the president.

She looked down at her handheld, flipped through the features, and found the entry form for the election to the presidency. Understanding the importance of what she was about to do, she placed her hand firmly on the screen. When she removed it, the screen flashed her name and Edward's as candidates. An election for president had officially begun.

Chapter 12
Michael

Fifteen cycles as a guard for the lower-level detention center all to end up as a prisoner in his very own department. It made sense given the way his last life had ended. Michael was the only one who had any actual knowledge of the time before the destruction, but no one would listen to him. They were all fresh, raw grows with no memories and just the base imprint to help Legacy back on its feet. It was customary for the system to grow a human to a certain age with the knowledge and experience required to perform their tasks. That's how they taught it in lower educational classes at least. He wasn't a first-generation human, so it was rarely talked about. He hadn't even seen a birthing bed before. From what little he could remember the sentinels were supposed to ease the transition into society but that hadn't happened this time. When he woke up he'd had all of his memories from before. That was different, and he needed to know how it had happened. He needed to know what Cade had done to him. He remembered some scientists talking about transferring memories into minds one time over a heated debate. How the process represented the ultimate backup plan. If all else failed, Legacy would grow a batch of humans and imprint them with the skills to perform the required repairs, but that would only occur if Legacy couldn't self-correct the issues. One scientist had declared the only way would be to manipulate the growth of the human mind, so the physical mind in the second body was identical to the first.

Cade had to be somehow responsible for all this. Michael remembered how he'd been trapped. Cade had probably set off the bombs or whatever explosions they'd designed in that makeshift lab of theirs. Chloe was involved too. He remembered seeing her in his last moments, lying dead beside him. So maybe Cade had killed her too just like him. But if she'd gone through the process like he had, wouldn't she remember like he did? Either she was acting, or she truly had no memories from before the destruction. She must belong to the rebel faction, but what part had she played? The first time he'd confronted Chloe after waking, she'd acted like he had lost his mind.

Michael closed his eyes, pinching his nose. His head ached. The feeling of the chair came back to him. The strap tight around his forehead. Cade was talking to him, mumbling about how his death served a higher purpose. That's what he remembered from just before the darkness overtook him. Before he…what? Died? Transferred? He wasn't sure what the correct name for it was, and to be honest he didn't really care. Well, if Cade operated that way, maybe he'd like a taste of his own medicine.

The system recorded everything. He knew this because he'd worked two full cycles at a post operating the surveillance systems. He'd been one of only a few humans who assisted that part of Legacy, which gave him a vantage point allowing him to witness events few ever did. He'd made sure to take advantage of that as well. From the core out to the satellite stations, he'd mastered Legacy's security mechanisms and made sure they functioned properly.

He knew Legacy would alert everyone if he broke out, but he recalled a way around the security. A way to trick Legacy. He was glad he'd convinced Tyre to bring him the handheld. Tyre had shown a certain level of creativity by using the girl as an intermediary when he was first placed in the cell. No one seemed to notice or care that she was helping him and Joshua hadn't asked about her when they first met. If he'd had visited minutes earlier he might have caught her giving him the handheld. He leaned back on the bed and pulled out the device from where it was hidden. The design looked like any handheld but inside, in the coding, it was uniquely different and powerful. He passed his hand over the wear and tear it had accumulated during its lifetime. He wasn't sure where it had been or who had even created it, but he knew it was a major part of what was going on. Its purpose might not be important anymore, but it had abilities that he needed. He remembered taking it. Chasing the rebel down. At the time he hadn't realized its capabilities. Even the tech he showed it to hadn't realized its full potential.

There was no way the device had been built by any of the techs he knew. Until that point, he hadn't thought devices like this existed. He'd worked hard to keep the device hidden from Legacy and his supervisors. There was no way to know whom to trust. Luckily, the device could be hidden from Legacy.

Tyre had found it where he left it: in his quarters, lying on the desk where Cade had surprised him. Luckily, it hadn't been formatted. The device would be his only way to escape from the cell. It would be useful after the escape as well.

When he pulled up the background jobs, the screen stated three hours remained before the software's installation and configuration would reach 100 percent. Called InfoSEC, it used algorithmic predictions to search and ghost any local, active access credentials. The device mimicked a person and opened most doors. The application opened any powered doors—even the cell door, as long as someone nearby had a device on their body and had access to open the door. Fortunately, human nature was such that the people who wanted to keep you locked up also had the power to set you free. This applied to any door except for those with the pedestals the sentinels used. Some areas in Legacy were too dangerous to access. Until the system deemed the areas safe, the sentinels would lock up the area with a door and pedestal setup. It had no dials, no buttons. Nothing. Michael remembered watching a sentinel use one of those doors. It had walked up to the pedestal and paused for a moment, and then the door had opened. If only he'd had the handheld at that point to record the signals for analysis. There were more to those doors than what the sentinels had told them.

One of the first mods he'd learned about was the open comm app that would link to local devices and use the secondary device to send signals to a destination device. Michael could send messages without being detected. If you queried the system, the message would read as if the person attached to the paired device had sent the message instead of him. Testing the messaging system proved there was no external trace of the messages being sent. There was likely some local trace to the device forwarding the message, but as far as he could tell, the app performed a purge of the message after it was sent. He'd thought surely they would catch him, but apparently there was nothing in Legacy's coding to detect any anomalies in the communication.

Michael knew no one would detect the messages he sent to Tyre or that he was the one to back him up even though he had no reason to. Michael had recruited Tyre not long after he woke to help hack Legacy. With so much of the system ungoverned by the sentinels, creating direct lines using unlocked handhelds had proven easy enough. Tyre didn't understand much, but he'd been useful. He'd helped with Richard, though thinking about what had happened afterward, he had to admit things did get out of hand. His teammates had always viewed him as a hard man to work with, but he'd never completely lost control. After he'd woken, though, any little thing would set him off.

Michael was more in control now and hoped to escape in time to pull the power before Cade, Chloe, or someone else remembered what had happened—especially what he had done to them—and finished what they'd started. Admittedly, there was some guilt over the backstabbing done when he started investigating the rebels. The pain of his best friend's betrayal was still fresh in his mind, but the sentinels had trusted him and given him privileges no one else obtained. He'd seen things. He knew things no one knew. If only he had more time to learn why the system tried to control humanity as it did. The guilt consumed him.

The door slid open, followed by a female's voice. "Hello, Michael. I'm Meredith."

Michael didn't recognize the voice. Not since he'd woken up or from before. She stepped up to the window.

Michael paused for a moment before responding. As a detention officer, he'd learned to add some silence when someone expected you to talk. It put them in an awkward position. They often didn't handle silence well. After a dozen seconds with her standing there watching him, staring and occasionally looking down at her handheld, he turned away to get some sleep.

Then she spoke. "Interesting."

He grunted, turned back, and sat up. "You're not going away. I would think you'd see I'm a little busy. I have a nap scheduled now and another for later. Then can you guess what's next?"

"A nap?" She pointed her finger at him.

"Exactly. So, what do you want?"

The woman looked down at her handheld before speaking again. "You don't like small talk. Very well. Do you know why you're here? In this cell? Do you remember what you did, or is it all a blur? As if dreaming or not fully in control."

What did she want? Yes, he'd done it. Yes, he'd felt more alive in those moments. More everything, but she was right. He never was in full control anymore, but wouldn't tell her. He didn't owe anything to anyone, especially not her. This stranger. Not after everything that had happened.

She continued, "Your past biological-profile stats are interesting. I want to show you something." She flipped the display. "Oh, it's okay if you don't talk. You can look, can't you? You're not blind, are you?"

He glanced at the display. It showed two streams of heart rhythms, one on top of the other. The top one showed sporadic and flagging alarms, while the other consisted of a stable wavelength pattern. "The first one here…" She pointed to the one that kept jumping around, going past acceptable levels. "is yours from the moment you woke to before you were shot by Cade." It was speeding through time. A journal of beats recording his actions through each pulse. "I checked and it stays like this almost the entire time. While this one—" she pointed to the other, which showed a steady heartbeat, "—is mine. Notice a difference?" She paused.

"After speaking with Joshua and Ashley, I suspect I know what Legacy was doing. It took a little investigating, but you were being injected with high doses of adrenaline when you connected to the system through the tubes. Have you noticed any changes in your emotions without any tubes? I did notice that you stopped connecting. What I wonder is why it was doing that. Why it thought you needed the added adrenaline."

There was more looking at the display. More clicking and more silence. She was testing his patience, and he wouldn't give her the satisfaction. How was this woman getting to all that data? Michael had guessed everything would be recorded, but he'd never found out how to access the data. Even with his modified handheld, he'd tried finding data like that but couldn't. It's hard to find data if you have no idea where to look for it.

"You haven't connected to the tubes since being placed in this cell. How are you? More in control?"

What was she trying to say? Could there be another way? Maybe breaking out wasn't the smart move. Maybe *she* might be the way out of this cell.

Her words triggered something inside of him. A truth he hadn't realized existed. Someone had intentionally modified the system for him. It had to have been Cade, from before. The realization triggered another memory of him in the chair before Cade put him down...something Cade had mumbled before he passed out. Something about lethal doses of adrenaline providing the best shot at success.

More silence, and then he decided to give her something. He shifted his body, glancing at the handheld to check InfoSEC's progress. Almost halfway. He just needed to get rid of this woman, do whatever she wanted so he could get back to the work that mattered. He needed to reach the new city. One thing he'd learned from his past was to rarely trust and always have a backup plan.

"What do you want from me? Why are you here?"

More silence, then she pocketed her handheld and gave him her undivided attention.

"Back on Earth, when the Legacy project reached the final days, the local governments began to fight with each other over who was in charge. Even though Legacy was privately funded, Earth's governing bodies insisted they knew best, the proof being how they'd handled Earth to that point, which was widely thought to be less than ideal, trust me. Then there were the ideological debates about implanting a person's conscience into another body, one of the largest hurdles for humanity to accept. Many countries declared cloning illegal, and negotiations were stalled until the core megatech companies of Earth united together to develop an independent nation in space. They sent a rocket to a local asteroid and set it into an orbit around the moon, declaring it an independent nation. After a decade of fighting, they finally gained their freedom from Earth and proceeded with developing the birthing process in Legacy. The legal terminology made sure to leave out any references to cloning. Legacy was designed to grow a unique human, and with mind-mapping technology a human would wake up with the ability to perform tasks never done before. With enough time we believed I.R.I.S. could develop the memory transference. It is an amazing form of technology."

She paused as if in thought, or maybe to decide whether to say something. "It's my technology. I earned a doctorate in cyberpsychology with a specialty in neuroscientific technologies. This means I understand how people think in a world full of technology and how their brain works on a physiological level."

She paused again to think for a moment, as if reflecting on some memories. "Sometimes breaking the rules and finding alternate ways to achieve goals can be a good thing, but you can't do it alone."

Michael was getting tired. His eyelids began to sag.

"The body goes through a shocking process at different stages of the restoration, the most severe being when waking up. From what I can gather, the damage to Legacy had a strange effect on your wake-up procedures. I've corrected that problem so you can connect knowing the injections will be at healthy levels. Aren't you feeling weak? You need to connect."

It was a trick. She was probably lying. "And what if I don't connect?" He leaned against the wall.

"You'll continue to weaken and be weak for some time. There isn't enough food to sustain your large frame, and you need more. You'll get sick, pass out, and we'll connect you anyway."

"You're lying. I can't trust you. You haven't been through what I've been through. You can't know. You can't know because you weren't there, but I was. And I remember. No one else does but I do. I need to be free. The sentinels are going to kill us all. We can't let them fix the system. Not until I've finished what I started."

His eyes were growing heavy. It was hard to tell how long she waited, but without him noticing, she moved from one side of the window to the other. He really needed to sleep. He kept getting tired since he stopped connecting to Legacy. He pulled together as much energy as he could. Enough to still sound strong and in full control. "You have a point. But now listen to mine. What you are saying is extreme, and hard to believe. Give me time so I can better understand, and I will help you."

He didn't want to connect, but his body felt weak. How many times had he slept? Maybe she was right. He could feel the difference from before. It was why he'd stopped, but he would need to connect again, at least until he could regain his strength.

Meredith said something to break his train of thought. He looked up.

"Think of it this way. If I'm wrong or lying to you, the rage will return while you're still in the cell. You're only going to hurt yourself. But if I'm right, you will have learned you can trust me and you'll be well on your way to recovery. And earning your freedom."

It could have been the lack of sleep or just the overall difficulty with comprehending what she was saying, but he felt more willing to give her the benefit of the doubt. It would be the only way to find out. If she were really on his side, she'd make a strong ally.

Without saying anything he walked to the chair and slid his bulky wrists through the holes until his arms were fully inserted.

"I can help you, Michael. No matter what happens next, I will help you."

The tubes snaked out and latched onto his arms almost immediately. He started to feel the weakness. It made him want to close his eyes and relax. He rested his head on the glass.

When he awoke, he was sitting in a chair, his head resting on a table. *Did they move me?* He instinctively reached for his handheld and found nothing but air. It was gone.

"How are you feeling now?" Meredith asked.

It was a different room, one of the interrogation rooms not far from the cells. The handheld was lying on the table next to her. He felt his only way out slipping from him. That device had been going to get him across the tunnel to the other side. So much for trust. He'd have to change his tactics. Without the ability to message Tyre, he would have to use other means. It would be nothing to overpower her. Nothing was stopping him. Nothing but the chance of losing a way out. Back into the group.

"We both got what we wanted. I wanted to see what you are hiding, and you wanted your nap," she said, tapping away at his device. How had she known he was hiding it?

"I'll give you that something went wrong because no one here seems to remember who they are or what happened. At no point was any of this—" she motioned around, "—a part of the plan."

Michael realized Meredith remembered Earth. She was the first to have a full mind map. All his life the sentinels had told them a malfunction had corrupted the stored data the initial imprinting was irretrievable.

She exerted confidence and remained focused. She didn't waver as most did when he confronted them. She didn't change her stance, her look, or her posture. She continued, "You need to make a choice, and you have two options. You can play along with this stubborn go-against-the-group philosophy of yours, which I'll add hasn't worked great for you. Or you can choose to help. You can contribute in a way that is beneficial to both you and the group. The question is, what do you want? What is it you are trying to achieve?"

Michael assessed his situation. She had information that had never been accessible. She seemed to understand more about the system. Maybe a mutual sharing of information would be beneficial.

"Well, what will it be?" she said.

He thought for a moment, and just as she stood up, he said, "It depends."

She sat back down. "On what?"

"If you're willing to discuss what you went through, maybe we can negotiate."

She remained unmoving. "Maybe we can negotiate, but you must admit I have the upper hand. I am here on this side of the table while you are there." She pointed to him, cuffed to his side of the table on the chair. "From what I understand so far, we are correcting issues and working toward restoring Legacy. I do not see the deceit you referred to. What is this great danger you feel that you, and you alone, can address?"

Now it was Michael's turn to pause to collect his thoughts. Was she the potential ally he thought, or was this another way to trick him? "You'll think I'm insane. Ian thought so when I told him. Ashley did. Everyone did, so I stopped saying it. You don't seem to be any different."

"I'm here, aren't I? I'm listening and asking, and I'm in a better position to help you than anyone else. But you've got to give me something, Michael. Something I can work with. I can work on getting you out of here if you make me believe."

At this point, without the handheld, she was the only option. *Be careful. It wouldn't be the first time someone hurt you. Trust her only enough to get what you need.*

"You have the unique advantage of knowing what your life was like before all of this. Back on Earth?"

She nodded.

"We don't, but I know things, and I need certain assurances. You might be able to tell me what all this was supposed to be like, but I can tell you what it was like before it all came crashing down. You need to ask yourself a question: Do you want to restore this system to what it was? Because if you do, I can't trust you. If you do, I am your enemy. Trust me. That isn't something you want. The truth is, if everything is restored, then we all die."

Her eyes flickered slightly. She was trying to hide surprise. She hadn't expected this. She held the slightest breath before exhaling. "I see we can help each other."

"I want out, and I want to be left alone. I need to do what I need to do without anyone disturbing me, but I need some help from people I can trust. Not Cade, or Ian, or Chloe. I can't trust them. I need people who want to make a difference, and the first thing I need is for everyone to stop trying to fix everything."

"See, you're not making much sense. You want us to let you go and blindly put our faith in you. To do what, if not to fix things? Why should we leave things the way they are now? Why not perform basic repairs?"

This was achieving nothing. Of course, it would help if he did know why the destruction had occurred, or who was controlling the sentinels. "If I knew I would tell you. I need to be out there searching. If you don't set me free you'll find out why soon enough, but by then it'll be too late." Michael felt frustrated trying to make her understand. He leaned his head back.

She continued, "There is nothing there to trade for your freedom. If you want out of here, some things need to happen. Give me something—anything to prove you know more than you let on. You can't make me believe you with nothing."

He'd been close to proving it when Cade knocked him out before the destruction.

"I'll tell you that the dream of taking charge of this community will end just like it ended before. Sure, there are plenty of sentinels solely designed to keep this place going, helpful and beneficial tools for the cause. But there are other sentinels out there that are not programmed to be helpful. They are not controllable, and they are smarter than any of us. Than all of us."

"Tell me. Do any of them look human?" Meredith flipped her handheld around, showing a sentinel designed as a female. She looked human.

He shook his head slowly. "Where did you find it?"

He had never seen this new type of sentinel. They were usually only humanlike in function, without reflecting the body so closely. This was new; this was different.

"Tell me what you know, and once I am elected, I'll make sure you earn your freedom." She stood before adding, "As long as you play nice. If you step out of line even once, it'll be over. The adrenaline fix you were getting does answer a lot and does make me sympathetic, but that only goes so far. From here on out you'll need to walk the line. We all need to live together here. We need to work together."

She probably thought that the community structure could still be established. *That's what we thought. If we just tried hard enough. If we worked hard with the system and relied on the founders, we would succeed. We would survive. But we were wrong.*

In a fit of frustration, Michael tried to stand and walk to Meredith, but the cuffs kept him sitting. "What

I know is that if we bring this system back online as it was before, the sentinels will not leave any of us alive."

Chapter 13
Chloe

The lights were off, all except for the displays from the handhelds. A cover was hiding something she could barely make out.

"And why are the lights off?" Chloe kicked something as she stepped into her lab. She bent down and picked up a device she remembered she had placed on a nearby table. "Did you need to throw everything on the floor?"

She reached for her handheld to override the command to keep the lights off.

"Wait. Don't turn the lights on yet. We think that'll wake it up again," Ryan said as he kept his hand on her device.

"We found it with some damaged sents that looked like they went through a fight," said a voice in the darkness. One of the men she hadn't gotten to know yet. She'd need to correct that. Pulling up her handheld, she identified his name as Mardel. He was large and reminded her of Michael a little—but a nicer version.

"One had his head ripped off. This one turned on and asked for help before turning off again," another voice said.

Chloe focused on the hidden thing. She stepped up, carefully reached under the cover, and ran her fingers along the smooth curves of its body. "It's a girl sent!" she squealed with a smile.

The outer layer was softer than she would've guessed. "Turn the lights on."

"No," Ryan insisted.

She gave him her stern face. He paused for a moment before reframing his declaration. "I mean, we need to be careful."

"Tell me what happened, and we can get a better idea," Chloe said.

They explained how they'd found the group of sents. How David had been inside and shined the light on something that caught his eye.

"Tell me, were all the lights turned off before the sent turned on? Was it completely dark when David shined his light on the sent?"

Ryan slowly shook his head.

"So, we can assume that the sent will only turn on if there is enough ambient light or if you point the light at one particular spot. The spot being somewhere near her head?"

Ryan remained silent. She could tell he was thinking hard. She pulled out her handheld and yanked the cover off the sent's feet, making sure to keep the neck and head covered.

Both Ryan and Mardel leaped back, but the sent didn't turn on. They returned to look closely at it.

It looked made of steel or metal, but when she pressed against its stomach, the surface acted more like skin and flesh. The material curved under her fingers, creating an indention that disappeared when she lifted her hand off.

Ryan started to look more comfortable. He took out his handheld and began a scan. She leaned over to read the data on the screen. The device showed a close-up of the sent's skin as he passed over her right knee.

"Wait. Go back."

He stopped over her knee, where there was the smallest of a wrinkle.

"Yeah, there." She reached out and set the magnification to the maximum setting. "The outer layer is tiny segments connected to each other." She touched the place they were looking. "See how the pieces bend and fold like skin?"

A tightly woven system of connected parts. It had to be the most amazing thing she could have ever dreamed. She started feeling every inch of the sent's body.

"What are you doing?" Ryan asked.

"I'm searching for a way to connect," she answered.

After a thorough investigation found nothing, she examined all wireless frequencies for any transmissions. It had to be turned off or put in some passive mode, waiting for a trigger.

The design seemed to be built to prevent any physical connectivity. She wondered how the charging process worked. The other sents had many places where you could connect to manage them. Each had a main port at the base of their neck, and one on the base of their spine which was truly unique. This one was very different from any technology she'd seen so far. Most of the devices in Legacy were made to be mobile. The sent must require wireless connectivity for all its operations.

Chloe thought for a moment. Maybe the sent's hands or feet acted as a contact point, and the energy would pass into internal conduits, filling up her power storage. "Why do you think she'll turn on if the lights are on?"

Ryan looked to one of the men. The taller of the three answered, "Well, when Zhang turned the power on in the main section, it was still dark in the room where it was. When we went in, the sent didn't move until David shined his lights on it. I think he mentioned something about seeing a small light shining in its eyes, or maybe the neck. He didn't know where the light came from." The man stepped toward the sent's head. "It happened so fast," he added.

She lifted the cover, looking at its eyes. A dim light shined from underneath. That would be a passive sensor.

The sent had to be designed similarly to other wireless devices, but those devices were searchable in the system. This sent, however, didn't pull up. Chloe identified Ryan's and her devices on Legacy using a map of node functions in her handheld, but she couldn't identify the sent. According to Legacy, she didn't log as an active device, as if she didn't exist within the network and was completely independent and unconnected. Chloe needed to find out how the sent's power system worked. She wasn't lucky enough for the sent to have a *Plug Power Cord Here* stamp on her back with an arrow pointing to it.

"I think I know how we can make a connection without activating the sent through lights." Ryan pulled out a device. "This device scans various layers of the body. It might work on her." A pause, "I mean it." Ryan looked at the naked female body, flushed, and looked away, even though she wasn't real and looked as if someone had painted a woman bluish-gray. Not until Chloe looked closer at the skin could she notice the subtle differences. "Can we find a uniform or something?"

"For her? I like that. Yes, she needs some clothes, but first, we need her working again." Chloe smiled. Some of her brightness had returned after many days of depression from thinking about the loneliness of Legacy and the haunting memories that were coming back to her. "Let's give the scanner a shot."

She watched as Ryan looked at the female figure. He hesitantly scanned its body and visibly relaxed when he started to focus on the results from the scanner.

"This sent is an advanced piece of tech. Look at the muscular structure."

"Does it label the type of material being scanned?" she asked.

"It isn't metal. The scanner is identifying synthetic elements, but a large percentage is unknown."

"Let's flip her over and check her spinal cord."

Once she was turned, the scan didn't take long. "The spinal cord seems to be designed with a series of small interface adapters just underneath the outer layer, and there is also a larger connector, similar to the ones on our bodies, at the base of its skull under the skin." Ryan placed his fingers at the point and pushed in through the thin layer of soft material. "Yeah, here it is. Right here."

Chloe placed her finger next to Ryan's and felt it. "Do you have a knife?"

"A knife?"

"Yes, a knife." She looked up and stared at Ryan.

Ryan turned, went to the corner of the room, and came back with a four-inch blade that he hesitantly gave to her. She proceeded to cut around the adapter area. For a moment she thought the material was too hard to cut into until she realized she hadn't touched it at all. The material transformed and stiffened under the knife's blade. No matter how hard she pushed, some force kept the tip a half inch away from the surface.

"What are you doing?" Ryan asked.

"I'm trying to cut a slit, but I can't," Chloe said through gritted teeth. "Something is exerting a force that is too strong for me to push against."

She relaxed, put the knife down, and brought her hand to the location. She was able to push against the connector. The skin had loosened again.

"Fascinating."

"Fascinating? What's fascinating?" the man next to Ryan asked.

"It has plenty of power. That was some kind of protective mechanism to keep me from doing any damage." She noticed the gun in the man's hand. "Here, let me show you."

She pulled at the gun, which didn't release from his too-firm grip. She stared up. He looked down, let out a breath of frustration, and let go. She stumbled back a few steps, realizing she had been leaning against his grip. She gained her composure. "Thank you."

"What are you about to do?" Ryan asked.

She quickly registered her ID with the weapon, then aimed. He got his answer from the sound of the gun firing, which was loud in the tiny lab.

"What in the world, Chloe!" Ryan pulled the gun away from her and handed it back to its owner.

"See? Nothing. I bet the pulse didn't even reach it."

"Must be a defense mode," Mardel said, managing to step closer, his curiosity getting the best of him.

Chloe smiled. "Let's turn the lights on."

"No! Really? The sent will activate. Not that I don't trust you, but sents don't like us very much." Ryan looked to the guy standing next to him for reassurance but received none. He turned back to Chloe.

"I'm sure we'll be fine," Chloe said, searching for her handheld to turn the lights on.

"You can't connect it to the system. What if it shuts down Legacy?"

"Or attacks us," the big guy said. "From what I could see, she moved fast when she turned on."

Chloe thought for a moment.

Ryan stepped in between her and the sent. "I don't think we should do this. Not without restraining it somehow."

Chloe gave him a mean face, but figured she should be careful. There was no way to know the sent's capabilities, and it would be bad if she attacked.

They decided that they needed to restrain the sent somehow in a room that was secure. She did know of a room at the end of the hallway that would serve the purpose. It would keep the sent farther from everyone else, only had one way in, and was mostly empty. They brought in a table and a few chairs. They decided to secure its wrists and ankles. Luckily, the prisoner accessories from the guards' room had handcuffs that locked in place when activated by a controller key.

After enlisting a couple of strong men to transfer and secure the sent, they made sure to keep her covered as she limply sat on the chair at the center of the darkened space. They were about to lock the handcuffs around each wrist and ankle when Ryan rushed in with a uniform. Chloe nodded in agreement, and they clothed her. The handcuffs automatically closed when they were in place. A guard used a key to finalize the lock by touching it to a sensor on each cuff. The key would also have to be used to open them.

"What do you think you're doing?" Cade's sounded frustrated. He pushed his way into the room and looked at the sent sitting in the chair.

Ryan responded, "We are going to—"

Cade looked to Chloe, ignoring Ryan. "You can't turn this thing on!"

Chloe's face flushed with anger, as usual when Cade was around. "We can't study or connect her to anything. The only way has to be to turn her on. All we can do is try. We think that once charged, she'll turn herself on."

"I think you haven't thought this through, so let me ask the obvious question. Will we be able to turn it off again if we need?"

She thought for a moment. "Probably not."

"And what do we do if once it's on, we can't control it?"

Chloe looked to Ryan, but neither of them had an answer. She had thought of the same thing but was hoping it wouldn't be a problem.

"We can destroy it," Meredith said, walking into the room.

"Destroy it?" Chloe asked.

Cade stepped back and nodded, his entire demeanor changing as he turned to face Meredith. "It might be the only option, but it could lead to a tremendous amount of damage. We would need guns."

"No! That is not an option, and I'll prove that we'll not have to do that." In an instant, Chloe grabbed her handheld and turned on the lights. Cade leaped forward to stop her, but he was too late. The lights blinded them until their eyes adjusted to the brightness, but nothing happened for a minute. Then two.

The sent shifted in her seat, correcting the slump she was in from when they'd set her down. She somehow seemed much taller than her tiny frame could have been. Her hands lifted but paused once the cuffs reached their limits. Then she returned them to the table. Palms down. She sat motionless until Ryan moved toward the door. As if she was taking in a full breath of air, her chest lifted and her head straightened. Her tight, rigid movements began to smooth out and look more fluid, humanlike, but she didn't lash out or attack.

"Okay, what now?" Ryan asked.

Chloe stepped around the table at the center of the room and knelt beside the chair. "She might need some stimulation."

Meredith stepped up to the table and paused when the sent looked her direction, her eyes still shut, as if she was responding to the sounds in the room.

Chloe reached out and touched her hand.

The sent opened her eyes and looked at Chloe. She appeared to be profiling her, looking first at her hair, then to her face, and finally down her body.

"Oh, hello there," Chloe said.

The sent moved her eyes to the table immediately in front of her and then to each individual, observing her surroundings, even looking down at her arms. Her right arm lifted until the cuffs tightened against her wrists once more. Her face showed a very human emotion of confusion as she looked at Chloe.

"Sorry about that. It's just a precaution," Chloe said.

"What do we call it?" Ryan asked.

"My name is…" She looked down at the uniform she was wearing then continued, "I do not have a name."

"We'll have to change that." Chloe looked her over and thought for a moment. "You're an android, so Ann?" She shook her head. "No, that isn't right. Maybe Andi." Chloe smiled, looking to the group that largely was ignoring her.

"Andi. I like that." Ryan said.

Cade interrupted, "What is your purpose?"

"Andi," Chloe added.

Cade stared at Chloe before amending, "Andi, what is your purpose?"

She looked Cade straight in his eyes and responded, "My purpose is to ensure the preservation of the human species in its natural state upon leaving the planet Earth and to protect the natural progression in dealing with any possible genetic variations."

"That's a mouthful," Chloe said.

"You are here to protect us?" Cade asked.

"I am." Andi nodded. The action was hauntingly human.

"What can you tell us about why this place is destroyed?" Meredith asked.

Andi looked down at her restraints. "Can these be taken off?"

Chloe glanced to Meredith then to Cade.

Cade stepped up to her; his face was full of concern and interest. "We cannot take them off at this time." He touched Andi's hand.

She didn't seem surprised. It almost felt like she was testing her limits Chloe wondered what kind of programs were operating behind those synthetic modules. What, in fact, was the reason for her existence? To Chloe, she was serving the same purpose as Legacy. What exactly did it mean to protect them as they had been on Earth? And what had that been about genetic variations?

Meredith walked over and stood behind Chloe. "Tell me. Who created you?"

Andi smiled, "Another one did." Then she began to tap away on the chair's arm.

"Who is the other one?" Cade asked.

"She is the woman in a flower dress. She created me and gave me life. I think I need to find her and save her." Andi turned to Chloe. Her face was filled with sorrow. "Will you help me help her?"

Chapter 14
Joshua

The vests and handhelds converted to something called solo mode once Joshua and Ethan walked deeper into the tunnels.

"No power here," Ethan whispered.

Without any nodes to maintain connection to the Legacy server, the only available information would be local to their sensors. Without that information Joshua didn't know for certain how he'd find David, but he quickly realized it wouldn't be difficult. A loud thud and the crumbling of rock made it easy.

"What is he doing? Is he tearing down a wall?" Ethan said.

They followed the curve of the hallway until they reached another cave-in. Joshua paused to listen to crashing sounds as a rock rolled down a small hill of rubble to his feet. Looking up, he saw David straining to move a boulder half his size. He was focused on his task, not aware of their presence.

Ethan stepped up close and yelled, "David! What are you doing?"

David stumbled backward, startled and confused.

"Why, Ethan!" Joshua snapped.

Ethan grinned with a shrug as he started to help. "I couldn't help myself. It was funny, and what's life without a little humor?" He continued to smile as he stepped up and helped David move another rock. Joshua shook his head.

David remained focused on the rocks. "I think I found something. I want to know what's on the other side of this wall."

Ethan and David stepped deeper into the opening and continued clearing a path. Drops of water were leaking from the bottom of a pipe, splashing softly into small puddles. The water pipes in this area seemed to be flowing in one general direction, most of which turned toward the opening David and Ethan were working on widening. A loud bang echoed through the tunnel. Nearby lights flashed dimly in the darkness, and after a flicker, brightened. A series of lights on their vests began to blink, and Joshua's handheld declared that it had established an active connection. He could see Zhang and his crew working in the medical laboratory. Joshua clicked on Zhang's ID and opened a channel.

"Zhang, the power is on. Great job."

Zhang's voice came over the handheld. "Yes, we were able to activate the power to this side of the level. The larger room and the other side still have issues with connectivity. We're working on that now."

"Okay, we'll continue to investigate the water issue. Make sure someone stays in your area in case we need help. I'll be checking in every couple hours. If I don't reach out to you, send someone down."

"Will do," Zhang replied.

"This place looks like a small battle took place here. Why would someone purposely cause so much destruction?" David started to squirm his way through the tight opening now available due to their labor. Ethan and Joshua followed. The question went unanswered.

Joshua had to take off his vest to fit. Once through, he slipped the vest back on and checked to see if he still had communication with the upper level.

"Hello, anyone up there?" he said.

A long pause drew out, confirming that they were no longer connected.

"Ethan, go ahead and leave your vest behind so it can broadcast the signal from in here. Okay? It'll give us a little more connectivity at least."

Ethan was visibly upset. "Really? Why me? Why not David?"

David was making his way farther down the path.

"Because you're closer. Just give me the vest. We need to stay connected."

Ethan wasn't happy but shrugged out of the vest and handed it to Joshua. After a few moments, the vest in the main tunnel connected to his and began routing information.

"Hello, does anyone hear me?"

Joshua followed a dot, watching what he thought was Zhang moving around.

"Joshua, yes. You're on the map, and I can hear you clearly over the comms. Most of the repeaters on this level are still operating. As long as the power is running through them, they seem to be rerouting the signal to the servers."

"We're heading into a side passage, and we'll likely lose connectivity soon. We'll be back as soon as we find out what's down here."

After minutes of struggling, Joshua and Ethan broke out of the narrow confinement of the rock walls and found themselves in another tunnel like all the others. Joshua shifted one of his lights to shine toward a nearby doorway that David was about to open using the access sphere. Apparently, the sphere had power and was able to provide authentication.

"Wait a moment, David," Joshua said.

David paused too late. He had already touched the sphere. The door opened as he turned to Joshua with his hands palms up. "Sorry."

"I wanted to be prepared." Joshua picked up his gun and pointed it into the darkness beyond, moving swiftly and efficiently to sweep the room inside for any threats. "We have to be careful down here."

They stepped closer to the doorway. Faint clinks lightly tapped nearby. The sound rang through the corridor.

"Did you hear that?" Ethan whispered.

"Hear what?" David asked.

"It sounded like clicking noises."

"It's nothing, Ethan."

David took one more step forward then jumped back. A small metallic thing scurried out and shot between David's legs. He yelped and tumbled to the floor, shooting his gun into the ceiling, causing debris to fall on them. Joshua stayed clear of the mess. The object had two legs and two arms, with rollers on the ends. At its center were a black sphere and what appeared to be a large camera lens.

"We need to catch it!" Joshua shouted.

David struggled back to his feet. Ethan jumped into the robot's path, reaching down to catch it but grabbing a rock instead. "What is that thing?"

"It's a small sent!" David shouted.

The sent shot up, riding the wall upward, then disappeared into a small tunnel.

Joshua shined a light into the opening, but only found emptiness.

"What was that thing?" David asked, finally getting to his feet. "It was so fast."

Joshua turned back to the room the tiny sent had come from. "I have no idea. Hopefully our cameras caught something. For now, let's just move forward. We need to get the water turned on."

As they stepped through the now-open doorway, the lights from their vests illuminated most of the entryway. After a dozen feet or more Joshua paused at the top of a flight of steps.

David glanced at Ethan. "I guess we go down."

The sides and top of the stairwell had conduits strapped to the metal framework. David pointed to a series of pipes to the left. "Those are the water pipes that I've been following."

Joshua noticed how other pipes were merging and running along one another down the stairwell. At the bottom they found a doorway, and even though they no longer had direct connectivity to the system, some lights were on. The door had no sphere and stood ajar. They tugged it open, the hinges squeaking and groaning as they pulled together.

Joshua led the group, gun in hand, to clear the area. David and Ethan followed close behind, each with their weapon ready. Their footsteps echoed, making it clear that the room was a vast space.

"David, can you work on getting the lights turned on?"

Joshua picked up his handheld and started trying different applications. One of them displayed a live image of the area around the device, but the software was having trouble accurately analyzing the sensory data. Walls were offset and not connecting to each other. Joshua shined his lights and realized what it was trying to define. He stepped up to one of the walls and felt the outward curve of what he realized was an enormous container. To the side he found some steps leading up. Once he was atop them, the handheld showed a room with dozens of tanks.

"I found an electrical box here. I'm going to try to turn the lights on," David said.

"Need any help?" After a long moment's pause, Joshua was about to head back when he heard a thud.

"Got it!"

The lights came on in sections. The thuds of David flipping multiple switches echoed in the chamber. "The breakers were all turned off."

The handheld flashed an update indicating connectivity to the upper-level network. That was good.

"This is the water-storage room," Ethan said, pointing to a sign that stated the fact.

Joshua made his way down and found a nearby display mounted on a wall. "David, can you get some of these interfaces working? Try to fix any alarms or errors?"

They started inspecting valves and checking for damage.

"There could be a clogged pipe somewhere," David said.

"Maybe," Joshua replied as he climbed onto one of the larger tanks and began pulling on the door hatch to open it. It took all of his strength to make it budge, then eventually loosen. Once he had it open, he shined his light inside. "Empty. The tank is empty. Climb up on the others and see if any of them are filled with water."

Ethan picked one tank, while Joshua moved to another.

"The displays are broken. I can't do anything with them. Zhang or Ryan will need to come down here." David started checking the tanks.

"Here too. Not a drop inside," Ethan said.

"Empty," David said.

Joshua had thought restoring the water would be a matter of opening a valve or unclogging some pipes, but the real problem was worse. The tanks didn't have water to send to their level. Where was the source? There had to be something supplying the tanks. They needed to know how Legacy was pumping the water. He shined his light around to locate where the water could be coming from.

"They'd be larger than the others, able to carry an increased volume of water." Joshua said.

"What would be?" Ethan asked.

Joshua pointed at a union of connections where the water was splitting off from the source.

"We need to find out where these lead."

The room was filled with hundreds of conduits, but most, if not all, led to two main pipes down on the opposite end of the room. They looked like they could accommodate the volume needed to feed into their smaller twins.

Ethan and David finished checking the tanks and walked over. Joshua stared at the two pipes, which were easily three feet in diameter, for a long, silent moment. He tapped one with his gun and heard a hollow ping.

"Walk along the walls. We need to find out where the pipes are going. We have to find the source of the water."

David started one way, and Ethan went the other. There had to be a way to the source. Joshua began to inspect the pipes for any markings or labels. Maybe if he could pull up a name or ID number in the system, Legacy might have documented where the pipes led to. It was a long shot though. The structure didn't follow any of the standard blueprints. For some reason, it had been uniquely built. Joshua wondered who would have wanted to make things different from the plans and why. He walked around another massive tank to discover the answer—or more specifically a way to find the answer.

"I can't find anything," David said.

"Me either," Ethan replied.

Joshua walked up to the pipe near the wall and started pulling on a valve over a hatch.

"What are you doing?" David asked.

"This is how we're going to get there."

They all worked together to open the hatch. It thudded against the pipe when the group let it go. He could fit into the opening. Joshua leaned forward, looked inside, then stepped back.

"Yes. This could work."

"Work? What can work?" Ethan asked, looking at Joshua and David.

"You want to go in there?" David asked.

"Unless you can come up with a better idea. I don't know a way that will show us where the water is coming from."

They all looked at each other, then back at the opening.

"Okay, I'll take this one, and you two take the other." Joshua pointed to an adjacent pipe.

"We should stick together," Ethan suggested.

"We need to go down both pipes in case they split up and head in different directions. Just get in, crawl until you reach another valve, and open it. There is a hatch-release handle on the inside. Pull the handle down and start turning it clockwise." Joshua showed how the handle was turning the circular wheel on top from the underside.

David nodded and started to open the second hatch.

"Really? We're going to split up?" Ethan said.

"Look, if you feel this is too much, you can go back. You wanted to help. This is helping," Joshua said.

Ethan hesitated, then turned and started pulling on the hatch door with David.

Chapter 15
Michael

Without the handheld, Michael had little chance of getting out easily, and he could only guess how Tyre would act once his messages went unanswered. Meredith couldn't have foreseen the consequences of moving him out of the prison cells. Michael knew this part of Legacy well, and was aware of its vulnerabilities. For one, there was no line of sight to the guards without them moving to peer through the small window of the door. False panels lined the ceilings in these rooms, and although he couldn't fit above the wall to escape, wires and cables supplying communication and power to the local area were accessible.

He remembered spending a dozen shifts as a guard in the cells. Routing prisoners from there to the interrogation room and back had provided plenty of time to learn the area. Often a prisoner would be left in the interrogation room for hours before a sentinel was assigned his case. He remembered a time when one guy had—purposely, they later discovered—broken the system law after finding out that his girlfriend was sleeping with a guard. Michael guessed he had been waiting for the right opportunity.

If he remembered correctly, the vengeful guy had been an engineer and known the workings of the power system. By the time Michael reached him, he had managed to cut the power from all but the main entrance, locking himself and the guard inside. The guy pulled the power line from the ceiling and managed to bite through a three-foot length of comm wire, then strangled the guard.

Michael had followed proper protocol, thoroughly documenting the event and filing it with his supervisors, then submitted a separate report to Legacy describing the design flaw the prisoner had exploited. As usual, his report had been logged successfully and ignored. But the process had required a thorough documentation of everything the prisoner had done. He'd even had to suggest ways to prevent similar events from happening in the future. Michael wondered if he could pull up that report. It would be more proof that the memories were not figments of his imagination.

He reached up to find the line that fed power to the door's sphere, if he could cut it, the door could be forced open, and with luck, the guards would not notice.

After two hours of him prying, the panel loosened from the ceiling without making too much noise. It took another hour to pull the wires enough to have an idea of which fed the local services. Michael could turn the relay sensors off, effectively shutting down comms to the area. Luckily, they'd placed him in the first available room, and all the wires that fed down to the other rooms ran through it. The problem was, if he tore the wrong cable and triggered alarms, someone would investigate. Things would become dangerous. He couldn't afford to hurt anyone else. Once he cut power and proved to them he really wanted to help, he would need to live with these people. He understood that. No matter who controlled the system, he didn't see how he would make a big difference without their help at some point. He needed them just as much as they needed him. Meredith was right about that at least.

He paused, hearing a noise and a voice nearby. A guard stepped closer to check on him. He dropped down and sat at the table. A few seconds passed, then a head popped into the window, glancing at him. They wouldn't dare open the door without reason. Michael had a solid foot of height over the tallest, and was more than fifty pounds heavier than either of them. He figured it wouldn't have required much to take them out if they hadn't had the guns. And if one of them happened to lock the outer door, he would need the handheld.

The guy stood back more than a foot from the door. Either he was smart to keep his distance or he was scared to death. Good. That could be useful. The guard saw Michael sitting at the table as expected, then proceeded to back away and disappear.

After another hour Michael spent tracing wires, the two guards appeared restless, pacing around aimlessly. This meant time was pressing. He went to the wires, separated the first one, and touched it against an exposed power wire he'd managed to cut by rubbing it against the edge of the metal frame in the ceiling. He'd learned during his interrogation that Legacy was programmed to prevent anyone from being permanently locked in an interrogation room. If power was interrupted or communications failed, the doors would revert to physical pressurized locks. Michael hoped that hadn't been corrected after the report he'd filed. He would find out soon enough.

Michael pulled on the communications wire and breathed a sigh of relief when no alarms sounded. The guards seemed not to have noticed anything either. The manual locking mechanism clicked.

The romantically challenged engineer had also exposed some other flaws. The door's design allowed for a thin loop of two-foot-long wire to slide down into the wall and grab a release that opened the physical lock. Releasing this lock would trigger alarms unless you cut the comm link of the sphere. Michael pulled some loose wire from the ceiling and slid it down just as the prisoner had done before. The wire caught the lock release. Now the orb would begin to flash, but without communication, the servers wouldn't receive any alarms. Michael pulled on the wire. As expected, a click confirmed the door's metal catch releasing. The sound was louder than he liked, but it just meant he needed to move faster. He pushed hard on the door and managed to open it enough to prove the sphere wasn't connected to the system. His fingers were just slipping through the opening when he heard footsteps.

"Miles, what's the red light about?"

Michael acted fast. He pushed hard and shoved his arm out through the narrow opening, grabbing the guy, then used his other arm to push the door open. Screaming with all his might, he managed to slide through to the other side. The door slammed shut after him.

The guy mumbled, but his words were hard to understand. They didn't matter. Michael hesitated. Meredith's cautious, feminine voice came back to him. *This is not the time or place to harm anyone. We all have to learn to live together. We need each other.* It repeated in his head. It could have been her words or the fact his mind was clearer now, but this guy didn't need to die.

The other guard, Miles, finally decided to act and shot once, missing and hitting one of the lights on the wall. Michael released his grip on the struggling guard, grabbed his gun, and turned and ran. Miles took off ahead of him toward the main exit. Michael was close, but not close enough. Miles made it to the other side and slammed his hands on the sphere to close and lock it in place. The door firmly shut, sealing him off. There was no way past this door, and now that they knew what was going on it was truly over. He'd failed, and he would never get out of prison. He'd be locked up for life—or worse, they'd kill him.

"Ha, you thought you had us, huh? Well, I'm going to bring back Joshua and some guys. We'll handle you."

Miles leaned into the window, looking to the side, then yelled, "Hold on, Kris! I'm going for help!"

"No, you're not." Michael stood up and grinned.

Miles pointed his gun at the door as if to shoot Michael through it. "You're trapped. You can't hurt me."

Michael stepped back and lifted his hands in mock surrender. "You've got me. I can't hurt you." He pointed behind Miles. "But he can. How's it going, Tyre?"

Miles spun to face the looming man behind him. With the flip of a wrist, Tyre removed Miles's gun, turned, and shot him with it. *Great, that's not going to go over well.* Tyre placed his hand on the door, but it ignored him.

"It won't open. It's locked. Try his hand. He might still have enough warmth in him to pass the authentication."

Tyre picked up Miles and dragged him to the door. He placed the dead guard's hands on the sphere, but they only received a loud beep and a denial-of-access alarm.

"Didn't think that would work, but it was worth a try. I need you to get Meredith. She has something of mine. Something she took from me. Find her and bring it back to me."

Chapter 16
Andi

    The humans were scared. The female named Chloe-147 kept referring to Andi as "her." She concluded this was part of why I.R.I.S. had installed the gender-identity within her programming. Humans go to great lengths to force their forms of identification on the unknown and foreign. The physical structure of her body was less intimidating and did seem to be helping with them accepting her. All biological readings presented micro-indications they were cautious but willing to trust her given the correct set of circumstances. However, the way they'd found her didn't present the best image of trustworthiness.
    Meredith-148 seemed more settled and controlled than the others. She appeared to be processing, suggesting she had assumed the leadership role within the group. The man to her right named Cade-148 was still kneeling and seemed genuinely curious about Andi.
    He leaned in, speaking softly. "Do you know why the other one created you?"
    "She created me for the ultimate purpose of protecting the human race. To stop those who would cause them harm and ensure the continued existence of your species." Andi spoke matter-of-factly, as if it was a truth everyone knew and should be aware of.
    He spoke again. "Can you tell us why Legacy has been destroyed?"
    She shook her head and tried to process why Cade-148 was following this almost random line of

questioning. Humans did seem to be insufficient data-gathering beings.

"Can you tell us anything about the destruction?"

"I am aware of some explosions that went off while someone attempted to abduct me…"

"Abduct you?"

"Yes, I was to meet the creator for my final implantation when it happened."

Andi triggered her emotion software to display the physical representation of sadness. The humans reacted in different ways. Chloe-147 responded sympathetically, while according to micro-data points, others showed signs ranging from trust to disdain. Chloe-147's response quickly flagged her as a likely ally.

"Your purpose being to protect…" Cade-148 looked around and motioned with his hands, "…us?"

She nodded in agreement.

Cade-148 stood. Without saying a word he walked over to Meredith-148. "I'm not sure what we should do. What do you think?"

Meredith-148 had stared for 8.4 seconds before her body relaxed and she lowered her head. "I think—" Meredith-148 looked to Chloe-147, "—Andi is not a threat. She seems intelligent and stated she wants to help. Is that right, Andi?"

Andi agreed. She did want to help, but in more ways than they realized. They showed no signs of posing any real threat toward her or themselves. I.R.I.S. had informed her of the existence of a threat. A threat that had been her primary reason for being created. She nodded.

Meredith-148's body movements indicated she spoke truthfully. Evidence suggested she could be trusted. Cade-148 showed signs of deception and layered thinking as he held himself partially hidden behind Meredith-148, mimicking her movement. Instead of nodding he shook his head slightly, indicating disagreement. She needed more evidence to establish where he belonged in the human societal structure.

"But for now, due to what happened recently with the sent on the lower level, I think we will need to introduce her slowly to the general public. A time of evaluation, you could say. For now, let's keep things as they are. I hope you understand, Andi. We recently had a sent kill one of us, so we are cautious," Meredith-148 said.

"I am familiar with the interaction between the sent and humans at the refinery level. Caution is advised and recommended according to my evaluation of the situation. My goal is to gain your trust and become a positive influence in your community."

Ryan-148 stood and started walking out. "I've got a request to help Zhang with a power problem."

Cade-148 leaned in and whispered into Meredith-148's ears. Andi's sensors picked up his vocal signals. "I think we should keep a few guards close by with guns in case something happens. To be safe. Can we talk outside?"

Cade-148 smiled mechanically toward Andi as he walked out of the room.

Meredith-148 started to leave, then paused. "Chloe, can you take a look at this?"

Chloe-147 extended her hand, grabbing a handheld device and placing the one she already had on the table nearby. "What am I looking for?"

"I'm not sure. Just look at it and see if you find anything interesting."

Meredith-148 smiled, then stepped out of the room. Chloe-147 started to leave but paused to address Andi. "It'll be okay. We just need to find a place for you. I'm going to talk to Meredith to see if we can move you. Okay?"

Andi watched the door slide closed behind Chloe-147, then scanned the screen of the handheld Chloe-147 had left on the table. With only three feet of distance, Andi used her internal visual software to flip the screen's view to orient toward her and then perform a keystone effect so her native programming would more easily interpret the software running on the display. In seconds, she began to use her transmitters to send commands to Legacy. Using the handheld screen, she monitored the system, allowing the device to act as the receiving side of her communication. She pulled up all the nearby nodes with sensors and created an audio pathway to listen through half a dozen nearby devices, including the handheld unit Cade-148 held. She sent the command to route all audio his device picked up to the handheld lying in front of her, keeping the volume low enough not to attract anyone from outside the room. She listened and documented what was said.

Cade-148 spoke. "We need to turn the sent off, or maybe even destroy it."

A pause triggered a command within Andi to initialize the video so she could get a visual on the immediate surroundings of the device and document body language for further analysis. They were standing a dozen feet away from the door, facing the opposite direction. Chloe was walking down the hallway, still looking at the handheld.

"Why?" Meredith-148 asked.

"We don't know enough. So far, sents have not exactly been our friends here. It could be dangerous."

"It hasn't shown us any reason to not trust it. I do agree that we need to be careful, but to get rid of it would be a mistake. We should be cautious, but seek information. We need proof. For instance, who is its creator? What did it say it was going to do? Its final implantation? This information is valuable, and if she is telling the truth, she might be a useful ally in helping us get back on our feet as a society."

The moment the door started to slide open, Andi terminated both the visual and audio streams. Chloe-147...no, Chloe. Andi's software reached the conclusion that the humans were referring to each other without the added numerical identifications, and therefore she needed to as well.

Chloe walked back to her spot near her handheld, still focused on the one Meredith had given her. Andi's concentration was split between monitoring the software and addressing her. Chloe began talking about tasks she would perform to take care of Andi and make sure everything worked out. The door slid open again and Meredith walked in, but instead of addressing Andi, she walked up to Chloe and motioned for her to step outside the room. She did so. Andi decided to connect to Meredith's handheld, which proved to be the better unit to pick up audio. Meredith was holding her device, so the video feed was pointing away and showed Chloe looking up to the taller woman.

"Can you tell if it's receiving any signals? If it's being controlled by someone else?" Meredith asked.

"Someone?" Chloe's physical actions indicated hesitation and confusion before she continued, "I can't tell you for certain, not without getting some scanners. I do have one in my lab, though."

"Go ahead and get whatever you need. It's important to know her abilities and limitations."

Chloe began walking away.

The door slid open again and Meredith stepped inside. Andi decided to communicate more openly with her now that they were alone. There was sufficient evidence to conclude that Meredith could assist with her integration into the community. She would begin by extending information to her. Information Andi knew she wanted to know. She could earn trust by voluntarily giving rather than waiting to confirm after they invested energy into proving or discovering what she could do.

"Meredith, I am not being controlled by anyone. I exist outside of the Legacy matrix. You are welcome to scan me and verify that I am speaking the truth. I will not stop you."

Andi's logistical software had calculated the best course of action was to reveal this part of her abilities, something they could discover with any rudimentary scanning device. Her software included a capacity to listen to conversations through any auditory device, but doing so would be an uncertain variable—as all things were when dealing with humans. The situation did present her with a favorable chance of gaining trust now that Cade was not among them. Once they discovered she could remotely listen through devices, they'd use the knowledge to plant false information in her database, which would make assisting more difficult. Her database stated in most cases when one entity encounters a more advanced counterpart, the inferior develops emotions of paranoia and defensiveness. The best course of action is to reveal the superior ability and allow time for the inferior to see that they will not be abused. Andi processed that the sooner they could accept her presence as an ally, the faster trust would be earned. It was crucial Meredith saw Andi as a benefit to all humanity.

Meredith opened her mouth, shut it without speaking, then sat on a chair at the table opposite Andi. "You could hear us," Meredith stated.

"I can, but you shouldn't worry. I cannot harm humans. It is not in my directive."

"Tell me, is the final implantation supposed to give you the knowledge you need to help us?"

"I am not directly aware of the details concerning the final implantation. I can only extrapolate that a final physical alteration was to be carried out, along with more software modifications."

Meredith reflected for a moment. She tapped at her handheld. Andi couldn't see what was on the display due to the angle and lack of reflective surfaces available.

"Does that mean you have basic functionality?"

"No, most of my available hardware functions are enabled. I cannot know if there is programming locked away from my awareness. I do have information stored in my memory banks."

Meredith's eyes widened. "What kind of information?"

Andi moved her arms. Her software continually adapted to mimic the human behaviors she witnessed. The cuffs pulled on her wrists. She looked down at them then back up, but didn't say anything.

The door opened once more, and Chloe walked in with equipment in hand. Andi identified the machine and pulled up information on that device. It was outdated. Something that would have been replaced a thousand years before Legacy left Earth. It was a basic frequency scanner that forced the user to dial through various frequency ranges to pick up any noise. The scanner would detect underlying wireless communication that was being transmitted and received through Legacy, but it wouldn't detect her audible inversion techniques. It might indirectly detect the signals if she tried some basic scrambling techniques to prevent detection.

But the communication they were looking for didn't exist because no one was controlling her. She was completely self-sustaining. They certainly wouldn't detect the telepathic communication.

Andi froze, processing heavily for a moment. The phrase telepathic communication had come out of her deep learning functionality. The process triggered her recurrent neural networks. It was an unknown variable in that section of her data being developed to allow her to make a conclusion. Something—or more accurately, someone—had telepathic abilities. Telepathic communication was typically attributed to biological creatures. For all created beings, it was comparable to wireless communication. If this new connection was, in fact, from a missing piece of her knowledge bank and there were humans with telepathy, she needed to determine if that process had naturally occurred or if it was a form of genetic manipulation. The Human Life Movement Act established by Dr. Witaford required her to provide adequate evidence as to the progression of such an evolutionary change. If contamination was found then she'd have to exterminate the modified genes or entities.

Chloe looked up. "I do not see any communication."

She wouldn't. Andi was devoting her processes to evaluating the potential of telepathy.

The door slid open, and a man walked in. Andi scanned all profiles to match his ID with what was stored in Legacy. She transmitted a command to show the identification on the handheld on the table in front of her. The information flashed a microsecond before switching back to the default display. His name was Tyre.

He leaned in and whispered in Meredith's ear. Andi's sensors again picked up the audible stream he produced.

"Michael wants to talk to you. He says that he is willing to do things your way."

Meredith stood a little straighter, took in a deep breath, and stepped out of the room.

A quick search revealed the detainment of Michael for abuse of another human. With the human species at dangerous numbers, all threats—even if that threat was a human—must be addressed. Michael was a threat.

Chapter 17
Joshua

Ethan entered the pipe and started crawling after David, giving Joshua some time to think. Ethan and David disappeared from his handheld. As far as his system knew, he was alone.

He tapped the top level and called up for Chloe. She didn't respond, so he tried Ryan. "Ryan. Can you hear me?"

"I'm here. How's the situation down there?"

"We found a room full of empty water tanks. I'm not sure how much power or signal is going to be available once we go deeper, so no one will be hearing from us for a while."

"Okay, I'll tell the guys down on level three. I'm headed there now."

"Sounds good."

The silent room stared back at him. Odd bangs and creaking sounds came from the levels above, the product of thousands of pounds of metal, equipment, and technology bearing down on him. Not to mention all the people trying to learn how to use the tech and perform various tasks. Down here he was the only one in a room that had nothing moving. No little sents creeping about and certainly no humans. If something fell on him, if another cave-in occurred, or if he had an accident, no one would know and they'd probably never find him. But he had to push forward, to move and find the reason they'd run out of water.

Shoving the gun to the side, he let it drag behind him in the pipe. He crouched down and started crawling headfirst. He shined two lights forward and one behind so he could easily glance backward. The handheld was still attached to the gun and read that he only had three hours of power left before charging was required. Noise echoed behind him through the narrow pipe. His shoulders rubbed against the edges, making it hard to see. Joshua thought of the little sent coming out of nowhere again. The tiny metal object hadn't seemed too dangerous.

He was suddenly aware that his breathing was the only noise being made. The pipe looked big enough for a casual shrug to move him forward. It almost felt smaller. Joshua settled into a routine of pulling himself forward with his hands in sync with his legs and feet, so his knees wouldn't scratch against the pipe. Reach out, pull, and shift. Reach out, pull, shift. He must have traveled a hundred feet or so before a soft sound crackled from his comm unit. He pulled the gun to him and disconnected the handheld. A warning confirmed he had no connectivity and that the unit remained in solo mode. The comm noise wasn't random static, but a pattern, almost rhythmic, but not quite. Like two in-sync tones dancing with each other, talking to each other. After a moment they stopped. He saw nothing, so he returned to his routine. He reached out then pulled forward while pushing with his feet. It didn't take long before he encountered another hatch.

He struggled to break the seal, then cracked it open. Seeing and hearing nothing, he widened the gap. Rust coated his arms as the lid screeched. He stopped with enough space to slide through and lowered the lid as quietly as possible. He decided to lock it down in case anyone or anything might pass and notice. Better not to be obvious. The area seemed to be another maintenance room. The pipe he'd climbed out of continued down a narrowing hallway, but the one David and Ethan were in was nowhere in sight.

The destruction hadn't reached this part of Legacy. Joshua checked his vest. Scars marked it from rubbing against the pipe, but it still appeared to be working. It did, however, declare one hour of use remaining, and still couldn't connect to any other devices even though power was in the immediate area. Lights shined overhead.

He continued to follow the pipe down the hallway, pausing to check side rooms to see if any water pipes were exposed. His muscles started to relax, then tensed as familiar metallic footsteps echoed close by. He paused, realizing he wasn't the only thing down there. The sound had to have been another sent, and he couldn't take on a sent. Not alone. He needed to hide, and quickly. The tapping grew louder.

Leaping over the pipe, Joshua lay on the floor and waited. Only seconds passed before the sent crossed to his right. He had forgotten to turn his lights off. One shined above him toward the ceiling. He tapped it off. The stepping paused, and sounds of distant noises echoed through the chamber. Joshua lifted his head to see that this sent's design was different. It was tall and thin, feeble, with a wide head twice the size of a human's. After a closer look, he discovered it was wearing an attachment that covered most of its head, but opened at the front. The sent shined a light against the opposite wall, scanning the pipes. He quickly dropped to the ground with a slight thud. The sent turned around and scanned toward him. A series of lights canvassed the area.

Nearby there was another step, then two more, almost on top of him. He held his breath and tried not to make a move. Not even blink. The steps paused again, but after a minute or two, they continued and faded. He remained still long after the sounds disappeared.

Once they were far enough away, Joshua cautiously stepped over the pipe and started to follow the sent. He would have wanted to avoid it, but it was traveling the same direction as the conduits. For now, he needed to keep an eye on it.

The distant steps led Joshua to another sent. A taller, skinny one similar to the one he'd seen earlier. He wasn't sure where it had disappeared to, but this one wasn't wearing the attachment on its head. It was making loud noises as it labored to move a large rock.

"Our estimation is that he's on the other side of this cave-in," a second sent said to the first. It was short, not nearly Joshua's height but almost as wide. It resembled a metal block with arms and legs.

"You said that already," the tall, skinny sent replied.

A thud echoed as the blocky sent punched the rock. The boulder cracked. Another blow caused it to break into pieces small enough to haul off.

"I know. I'm reporting the latest data coming from our scans of the area. We are still unable to locate any working sensor bots, so we will need to do this manually."

The distinct desire to turn back came over him. He needed to let everyone know that there were sents down here. He turned to go back but stopped when a third sent appeared, coming from that direction. With no place to hide, he had to push forward. There had to be a way to go around the sents. He saw more pipes he could hide under.

The squat, bulky sent dropped a boulder. He let out a grunt. "It's going to take months to clean up this mess, you know. And who knows how long to perform the repairs needed after this massive mistake? Why don't they let us head up to the top—"

"Your job is to work, not think," the tall sent interrupted. "Now, start clearing the rubble."

Joshua heard the third sent getting closer. Soon he'd be found.

The blocky sent turned, vaulted into the air, and punched a boulder that was stuck about ten feet up, causing a small avalanche. A cloud of dust filled the area. Joshua ran to the pipes and slid underneath with one quick motion.

Just as he settled down, the third sent walked in. This one was like the first, tall and skinny with the larger head. Maybe it was the one that had almost caught him.

He waited to see if they saw him, but they didn't notice him. They both turned and stood tall with their arms to their sides, speaking in sync with each other.

"Sir."

"Enough with the formalities. I'm old and don't have time for this. I need my delegra. It'll take too long to start with a new one. I've worked too hard to lose him now. He was close, and if he doesn't get into the next session soon, a lot of hard work will be permanently undone. How is the progress going?"

"Sir, we should be through in another day or two. We are working as hard as we can," the tall sent reported.

Why would sents communicate like this? Joshua would have thought that they wouldn't need to communicate verbally. Wouldn't data just be gathered and transmitted to a storage unit? And why was the sent asking questions as if it didn't have access to the same information as the others? The other two acted like they were subordinate to the new one, and that one sounded different. His voice was weak and cracking. This all made no sense. They were searching for someone, for a delegra. What was that?

"I will report this to Capro. He will not be pleased with the slow progress."

"You can tell him that he can come down and help us himself. We've been working for ten days straight with little to no rest," the blocky sent murmured.

"What was that?" the weak sent asked.

The other sent stood in between them. "Nothing, sir. We will double our efforts and reach your delegra within the next twelve hours."

"Ah, well, that is noteworthy. Be sure to bring him directly to me. It is urgent. I will make my rounds and come back to check on your progress."

The thin sent started to walk away, toward Joshua. He slid farther under the pipes against the wall while the sent walked back to where he'd come from. He couldn't go that way anytime soon.

"I'm going to make sure the report gets filed," said the tall, skinny sent.

The worker sent said nothing. It returned to the rocks while the taller sent stood and watched.

Hopefully, David and Ethan were having better luck.

Joshua had a good angle to watch the two remaining sents working. He watched the skinny one head down another corridor and into the darkness. The larger sent that was doing most of the work continued its way through the cave-in, creating a tight opening at the base where rocks piled up. Joshua could have shot it and caused another cave-in, this time trapping the sent in the rubble. But the gun might not be powerful enough to do anything more than stun someone. There was no way of knowing. Still, if the sent got stuck in the rocks, it could buy him the time to cross the room and find a way back to the top.

Whatever he was going to do, it needed to be now, before more sents came by and before his opportunity had passed. He was wasting too much time.

Chapter 18
Meredith

Meredith thought through the different reasons Michael might want to talk to her. Maybe he'd changed his mind, but she didn't think he was playing games. He'd acted more…direct. How he, out of everyone awake, understood so much confused her. She remembered Earth and the way things were supposed to be, but he seemed to have a grasp on what had actually happened to Legacy, which was far from what she would have expected. Something had taken a turn for the worst, and she needed his knowledge and information to correct the problem.

Being so focused on the glaring problems it took her a while to realize Tyre's hands were gripping her elbow tightly. The idea of what was going on didn't settle in her mind until she tried to pull away from him.

"Stay close and don't say a word," he said.

"What are you doing?" Her voice grew increasingly louder. He squeezed tighter. It felt like he was going to twist her arm off.

"Listen. We need the handheld. The one you took from Michael. Do what I say, and you'll be safe. No one will be hurt. Well, no one else."

This was certainly not good. Why did this guy want the handheld? "Well, if you want the handheld, we are going the wrong direction."

They paused, and she pointed back toward Chloe's lab.

"Where is the device? And don't think to try anything. I could snap your neck in a second. One false step and I end your life and possibly others."

Her knowledge of the way things should be did not reflect Michael's unique perspective. It could be possible Michael had something that could help her. She felt lost, her mind raced to catch up to all the moving parts that were in play. Maybe the best approach was to give him what he wanted. For now. Even if he got the device and did whatever he wanted. There was nowhere he could run. This place couldn't be that large.

She focused all her energy on projecting a calming and submissive appearance. "Okay, I understand. I want you to know I will comply."

Tyre's hard face only grew harder. "Yes, you will." He pulled out a handheld from his uniform, tapped, and spoke. "Meet me at this destination point. Michael needs you to help him."

A pause. "Okay, I'm headed there now." Tyre pocketed his handheld.

They turned around, heading to Chloe's office where she often stayed. Anything to buy more time to think through the best steps to take without anyone getting hurt. The vacant tunnel provided no options for her. Most people were probably congregating in the mess hall to eat. Bad timing. Tyre had likely planned things that way. She needed to be ready to take advantage of any opportunity.

She started to walk down a side hallway which would hopefully lead her to a group of people, but he stopped her. Turning, she realized he had a handheld. Chloe's name blinked, declaring her location. So much for him being easily distracted. This would not end well.

They finally arrived at Chloe's lab, having backtracked most of the distance from where they interrogated the sent.

"Do I need to remind you what's at stake?" Tyre asked.

"I'm going to retrieve the device. At that point, you can do whatever you need to do with it. I am cooperating fully."

Tyre gave a serious stare, then a slight nod.

She took a deep breath to relax her nerves. After she pressed on the sphere, the door opened, revealing an energetic women hard at work on some strange device with an organic material covering it. Chloe's eyes darted back and forth between the device and a nearby instrument, not noticing their presence.

Meredith choked when she tried to speak. "Chloe." She looked up to Tyre. He nudged her forward, causing her to shift on her feet.

"Chloe, do you happen to have the handheld?"

Chloe ignored her for a second before looking up. "Meredith. Hey. What?"

"The handheld I gave you?"

"Oh. Here it is." She picked up a handheld. "No, that isn't it. I know I put it somewhere. Wait a moment."

Raising a hand up then shuffling through broken pieces of hardware, Chloe started picking up broken handhelds and tossing them on a side table. "I meant to start looking at it. I was distracted with this…this thing. Let me take a—"

"That's okay. Something has come up and…" Meredith paused to collect her thoughts. Chloe was still unaware anything was going on. "Well, I need it back."

"No, it's okay. I can look at it right now. I don't mind. I was running an analysis software when I remembered that the—"

"Chloe!" she yelled. Her right hand stretched out in a stopping motion.

Chloe's eyes widened. Her mouth gaped, then shut tight.

"I meant to say it is quite alright. I have some…" She shifted a quick glance to Tyre. "…testing I would like to perform. I'll give it back to you once I'm done, Is that acceptable?"

"You seem a little…" Chloe glanced to Tyre and back to her. "…off." She took two steps toward them. Tyre stiffened.

"There it is!" Chloe walked over to a table near the door, where she must have placed the handheld when she first came into the room. She picked it up and looked at it as if to confirm that it was the handheld they wanted.

Meredith nodded. "I'm just tired. I'm still weak from waking up. I'll head to bed when I'm done visiting with Michael."

"Sure. Whatever you want." Chloe glanced up at Tyre. He shrugged. She passed Meredith the device.

"Thank you. I'll return this once I'm done. Okay?"

Chloe sat back down with a confused look. "All right."

She turned back to the device she'd been working on before. It had a familiar design, but Meredith couldn't quite place it. Tyre motioned for them to leave. They turned and proceeded back toward the interrogation rooms. As they left, a new man was standing guard outside.

"Stay here and make sure Chloe doesn't leave the room," Tyre ordered, turning to face Meredith.

"Don't think I didn't pick up you mentioning you were going to Michael. You're pushing your luck. It wouldn't take much for me to hurt you. Some of these rooms are far enough away that no one could hear you scream. Your body can comfortably fit in one of those sealed containers. They wouldn't find you until we're long gone."

Tyre pulled the device away from her. She raised her hands in surrender. There was no reason to think he was bluffing. "I understand. I'll do whatever you want."

Until they were gone? Where were they going? Where could they go?

Tyre nodded, and they continued walking. Luckily they would have to pass through the mess hall to reach Michael. That would be her best shot at getting someone's attention. Maybe make a run for it into a group? Get enough attention to overpower Tyre?

As they reached a large chamber, Tyre pulled on her arm, forcing her to follow him along the outer curve of the domed room. It was mostly vacant, save for a small group of people talking in the center. She could have yelled, but as if he was reading her mind, he gave her a painful squeeze. "Don't think Chloe is safe. You make a move or do something I don't like, and my man will kill her slowly. Remember that."

She realized she might not have a better chance, but with Chloe's life on the line, the safest bet would be to play along, knowing whatever happened next should be fixable. She had been a part of the project originally and assisted with the software development. If they could activate some sents, people like Tyre and Michael wouldn't be a problem. Either they would obey the law, or as much as she would hate to do it, they would suffer the consequences.

They were just entering the hallway that led to the security wing of Legacy when Cade's voice called out from across the large room, "Meredith."

They paused. Tyre gave her a squeeze to make sure she knew not to let on that anything was wrong.

"Cade, is it?"

He nodded.

"How can I help you?"

Cade glanced at Tyre before starting. "I wanted to give you the latest update on the water situation."

"Did something happen?"

"I was monitoring a connection from three levels down. Some techs are working on repairs to restore power and functionality to that level. Joshua found something. The last packets of information from his vest showed they entered a room full of tanks. It looks like a reservoir of water. The connection was lost, however, so I'm waiting on a response from them. They likely are too far from an active connection. Eventually one of them will pass by a node, and they'll reach out to us. I'll send you the data on your handheld."

He pointed to Michael's handheld. "What's the node ID for that one?" He picked up his handheld and started tapping.

"Meredith, we need to go," Tyre said. He was trying to end the conversation.

"Oh, you have two handhelds? Let me identify which one is yours." Cade was flipping through the screen.

"Yes, here are your IDs. I'll send you information as I learn it."

Meredith knew this would be the last time to get a message to anyone. She couldn't think of anything Tyre wouldn't understand.

"Keep an eye on Andi and send any information to Chloe, okay? She'll know what to do. Make sure she stays in the loop."

Cade nodded, turned, and walked away. Maybe he'd meet with Chloe and make the connection.

Tyre pressed the sphere. The door slid open. "Come on. Michael's waiting."

She stepped through to the other side.

Their footsteps echoed through the silent hallway as they passed the empty prison cells. It was only moments later that Meredith noticed the red stain on the floor and streaks toward the wall. A man lay folded over near the door in a pool of his own blood. Some of the blood was on the sphere that led to the common area of the interrogation rooms. The door's window was cracked open. Small shards of glass were on the floor in front of her. The lights on the other side were turned off.

Then she heard the familiar deep voice. "Did you get it?"

Tyre stepped up and passed the handheld through the window. It disappeared into the darkness.

She wasn't sure what she was about to see. A part of her thought she'd see some monster. Images of her childhood nightmares flashed before her eyes. She was frozen with fear as the sphere turned blue, then green, followed by the door sliding into the wall. She wanted to close her eyes, to run away, but she couldn't.

Michael stepped out, his fist bruised and bloody. She saw a man curled against the wall behind him with his head down. He looked up with pleading eyes. At least he was alive.

"We need to go to the power station," Michael said, then started tapping away.

"What do we do with her?" Tyre asked.

"Take her."

Chapter 19
David

David's muscles ached, and he desperately wanted out of the pipe. After what seemed like hours of crawling with Ethan's constant whining and complaining about how he couldn't breathe and wanted to go back, they started to take a gradual right curve for a few hundred feet before David finally saw the next hatch.

Once close enough, he shined his light on the handle and started to twist, but it didn't give. They worked together to force it open. The hatch made a loud noise as it slammed against the pipe.

"Could you be any louder?" Ethan snapped.

"I'd be a lot quieter if you weren't so useless," David replied.

Outside, he didn't know what to do, but they needed to be absolutely silent. He carefully stepped over some loose pipes lying in front of him. A loud bang and squeaking came from behind. David turned to see Ethan shutting the hatch.

Ethan glanced back. "What?"

David started, not knowing what he could possibly say that would make a difference. He shook his head and walked away.

"What?" Ethan asked again.

"Quiet. Try not to make any noise, okay?"

David had assumed he'd be able to find Joshua once they were out of the pipe, but there was no sign of him or the pipe he'd used. Just more smaller pipes, hallways, and rooms—dozens of rooms lined one after the other, with long hallways connecting them like a web of tunnels with no logical flow. The difference in structure caused David to pause. Nothing was spherical or cut out in the shape of tunnels except for the pipes. The rooms had sharp edges, flat ceilings, and were mostly square. Starkly different from the upper levels.

"Where do you think Joshua is?" Ethan asked.

"I don't know. We need to keep moving forward and find the source of the water."

The water pipe continued to curve, hugging a hallway, then straightened out, arriving at a dead end.

"I don't want to go back through the pipe," Ethan said.

David understood, but if they couldn't find Joshua or a way through, the pipe would be their only option.

"Start looking for a way around to see if we can find the pipe on the other side," David said.

They searched room after room, each having little odd differences, like one computer would be on one side of the wall while another room had it on the opposite. One had a computer built into the ceiling, treating it as a floor. It even had desks mounted upside down. Who would use a computer on the ceiling? Legacy must have been constructed with the idea of having thousands of people living and operating it, but there were no people in sight. Not alive nor dead, anywhere. It gave him an uneasy feeling.

"I found it!" Ethan shouted.

"Keep it down," David whispered. Their voices bounced off the walls and rang through the corridors. "We have no idea what's down here. What if there are more sents? We need to be careful."

He checked his gun. The stored energy meter had reached critical levels. An alarm ordered user David to charge soon. He had maybe one more shot. Why had he shot the ceiling when that tiny sent lunged at him?

Sets of ladders and walkways allowed them to follow the pipe. From the looks of these intersecting pipes, which were growing larger, they were getting closer to the source.

"Where do you think Joshua is?" Ethan asked after a long, silent moment.

He wouldn't stop talking, always mentioning or stating what was going on, or pointing out something he noticed like another empty room.

"David, I found another room," he said.

At least he wasn't shouting anymore. He was persistent and scared, which made David think he shouldn't have been down here. He was helpless and vulnerable, but that needed to change. They would both return to the upper levels heroes. The only thing to do was restore the water flow and direct it to the top level. The price was too high to go back without doing so.

They took more turns and a set of steps down, following the pipe's general direction. Then a soft tapping echoed through the hallway.

"What was that?" Ethan whispered

David could hear the fast, quick clicks of something hitting metal. Whispering, he leaned in close to Ethan. "I think it's coming from that direction." He pointed down to the lower level and started heading toward it.

Ethan paused and lagged farther behind David as he advanced. David looked back and motioned for him to follow. Ethan shook his head, but started to move when David walked toward him angrily. "You are in this now. Be a man and help me do this."

They climbed down a ladder and followed the clicking. It was steady, almost rhythmic. Tap, tap. Tap, tap. They slowly stepped toward it. The sound was close and didn't seem to be moving. It was just around the corner. Raising his gun, finger on the trigger, David took one last deep breath, then leaped into full view of what he knew would be a fierce sent bent on killing them. He fired his weapon blindly into the darkness. A loud explosion of a pipe bursting shocked him. Water rushed out, soaking and sending them to the metal flooring, not sure what was happening.

David started to get up, but Ethan pulled on him, trying to gain his own footing. They tumbled back to the floor.

"Quit pulling me down!" David yelled.

"Help me up!" Ethan shouted over the pouring water.

The gushing water quickly slowed to drips.

David pulled on Ethan, but again fell, slipping on the slick surface. He fell on top of Ethan, and they ended up on the floor once more.

"Sorry," David clamored. They were drenched from head to toe.

"Good job shooting that pipe. You've saved our lives."

They looked at each other, smiled, and laughed.

Chapter 20
Chloe

Chloe was determined to find the purpose behind Andi. The sent must be unique. She understood that much.

The scans confirmed that nothing and no one controlled her. The system viewed her as an entirely independent entity. Legacy didn't recognize her as a node, thus Andi couldn't connect to Legacy like the other devices did. It treated her no differently than a human.

Finding someone using a device was easy. You located a person by searching by their name, because they'd be carrying a handheld or wearing a vest. The device recognized and identified the last registered profile. If a device was left behind, the software would state the user was still there until they touched another device, triggering the auto-association feature. But she wasn't a device. Chloe wondered what would happen if she paired with a device. Would Legacy assign a profile to her as if she were human? If so, then they could track her and know where she was. They could mount a device to her somehow. It seemed clear the sent didn't communicate with Legacy in the same way most devices did. However, a connection could still exist between her and Legacy in a way that circumvented the tracking software. If so, that would make documenting her actions at any given time difficult.

Andi was still in the room where they'd left her, and the cameras showed her sitting idle as any person would. The lights were on, which would only happen if a person was in the room. Chloe noticed lights always turned off in a room when everyone left. She thought Legacy shut down the power. But the lights were still on where Andi sat. Legacy must consider Andi to be human.

"What's the purpose of a sent you can't control?" Ryan asked with his head focused on a screen as he walked in from a secondary room in her lab.

He seemed to be thinking the same things she was. Why would anyone build a system that couldn't be directly manipulated at a software level? There was no way to access her code and no way to learn anything about her without communicating with her external sensors.

"I'm not sure. What if we're simply not aware of how to control her?"

"You think we don't have the right kind of tools to communicate with it?" Ryan asked.

Chloe stared at him.

"With her." He rolled his eyes.

She smiled. "Exactly. I wonder if we're missing something."

"Wait, I think I remember seeing something around here. Like your scanner, but different. Let me see if I can find it," Ryan said.

He started moving things around, picking up tools and checking them, only to not find the device. "Oh, I'll check Cade's office. I'll be right back."

He was probably right. The sent might be programmed to only respond to certain commands or a specific manner of communication. Possibly a higher frequency her scanner couldn't detect. Maybe she used a form of dual-frequency communication or even a neural link that allowed transmissions to go undetected. She was obviously very advanced. Chloe thought that if she could trust Andi, she'd be the best way to get Legacy up and running.

Chloe remembered her dream and was thinking about it when something clicked in her mind. Something familiar about a neural link or a quantum bond between two devices. An image appeared in her mind so strong it knocked her to the ground. She clenched her entire body, her muscles tense, her mind frozen. When the pain released, the lab disappeared. She was back in her dream, in the same room her dream had ended in.

She looked to Cade, then down at herself. Her uniform had multiple colors running along the outer layer. Her instincts were to wipe her face for some reason, and when she did, she drew tears from her cheeks. The wetness sent a chill up her spine. The room was warm.

An older version of Cade stood in front of her. Much older, looking sad or angry. Why would he be angry? Why did his emotions matter, and why did she feel tears running down her cheek?

Then she spoke. Again with the feeling of not actually being the one speaking. Just an observer, not remembering but living out the actions for the first time.

"I watched him die. He's gone, Cade," she said.

Chloe walked into a nearby room to find Michael passed out and strapped to the chair next to Joshua also on a chair. She turned to Cade. "What did you do? Why is Michael here?" she shouted.

Straps bound Michael to the chair. Cade raised his hands in defense. "He found out about our plans. He was going to turn us in. I had to act, or it would be over."

"Joshua's dead, and he'll probably not remember a thing. We haven't had a successful test yet. Look around, we're done!"

Cade defiantly stood his ground. "Not yet. I can figure this out. We can figure this out. We need more time. Someone wants to help us. I just need to find them."

"Cade! Killing Michael isn't going to help anything."

"No, I've made some progress. I can do this. I just need—"

"Cade!" Chloe interrupted. "The bombs are in play. More will be going off in an hour. There is one last thing to do. We can try again next time. Hopefully, we'll have better luck."

Her heartbeat quickened. She walked out of the room, then woke up back in her lab.

"...put it right here. Chloe? Are you in here?" Ryan asked, looking the room over until he found her on the floor. Her mind struggled to make sense of her surroundings.

"Chloe. Are you okay?"

She could hear him talking but his voice echoed, as if he was talking through a pipe or maybe screaming from the other side of a wall. She worked to focus. His voice cleared. Her vision came to her.

"I'm okay. I think I..." Chloe shook her head to shake the murkiness within. "I don't know, but I'm okay."

"You don't sound okay."

Ryan helped her to a nearby chair, where she continued to gain her composure. What were these memories? They were real, yet disconnected. Dreams she had no control over. She put on her best fake smile. "I'm good. What did you find?"

Ryan paused for a moment before continuing, "I've got this device which detects all kinds of signals. There's a bunch of symbols. Like this one. I have no idea what SQRF stands for, or what it does."

"Sympathetic Quantum Resonant Frequencies," she said without thinking.

Ryan stared at her strangely. "Sympatheta-what?"

Knowing what the letters meant caught Chloe off guard. The meaning came to her like breathing. She knew this device could do what she needed. Not only that, but the SQRF device could affect those signals and repeat them, even change them, ghosting them to make it look like they'd come from the source transmitter. How did she know all this? The device felt familiar to her touch.

"Where did you find this device?" she continued.

"Someone found this a couple floors down. It was lying on the hallway floor as if someone dropped it there. I brought it up because it looked important."

Her fingers traced the knobs, then she remembered her dream. It was similar to the device she'd left behind when she was running for her life. Or was this the same device? She flipped the switch that read *SQRF* and recognized the familiar signal displayed on the screen.

"Can you show me where this was?"

Chapter 21
Michael

Michael wasn't sure if it was one or two terms after he first joined the security forces that he drew the short end of his team's responsibilities to guard the power plant, and hated every minute. He'd been young and willing to do whatever it took to make a name for himself. To prove to everyone that he belonged. At the time he hadn't cared much about the power system, but he had paid enough attention to learn the important things. Now he was glad. The overseers had talked obsessively about the system. How without the direct connection to the planet's core Legacy wouldn't work. They'd had conflicting ideas they wouldn't dare vocalize too loudly, but he had heard whispers about why the system didn't use the sun's energy. Others would say it did, but humans couldn't reach the surface. The sentinels had locked the surface away. The notion seemed absurd, but sentinels were able to do anything humans could do, so why put a person in danger when a sentinel could take his place? The power drawn never did add up to what the system produced. Either way, you couldn't spend any amount of time around the power plant's overseers without being dragged into a laborious tour of how each part worked. So he had a general understanding. Enough to make the plan work.

Legacy had secrets few were aware of, but he'd been able to discover his share before everything went bad. Emergency hatches and panels were hidden from sight for what he assumed to be aesthetic reasons. If you had the floor plans or were familiar with where the access points were, you could travel through Legacy unnoticed with a handheld. In this case, the interrogation rooms sat opposite of where he needed to be, and the power plant was far from the tunnel to the city entrance, where supplies and tools would be available. But answers were all that mattered. He had to discover what had happened to Jessica. Was she still alive? Why had they taken her? Or had she died like the sentinels said?

His throat caught, remembering her. Thinking about the loss and anger. It felt like another life, and in a way, it was. Legacy kept offering more mysteries with every secret revealed. One scientist had suggested I.R.I.S. was malfunctioning. One of the leading theories defined a rogue coder involved in the building of Legacy, leaving some people to wonder about the logic behind the rules and regulations being enforced. Michael had his doubts, thinking it felt more like someone was behind it all. He planned to find the person and kill him.

I.R.I.S. technically could still be active and operational, but unreachable from this level. However, if they couldn't reach her, the sentinels shouldn't be able to either. Someone else must be controlling them. How long ago had I.R.I.S. lost control of the sentinels? The core system might not ever have been built, as strange as that would be. There was really only one way to find out, and it meant going to the remote city. Especially the locations isolated from humans after what happened. After the accident took Jessica. She had just enrolled to be part of an in-depth scanning project meant to extend the new city. The first of its kind. Finally, a place where humans would have real room to spread out.

Then it happened. The sentinels flagged the area and stopped allowing human interaction. He was betrayed. It happened so fast he didn't know what hit him. He could still remember the shift before the accident, the last time he saw Jess.

Now nothing would stop Michael from finding out what had happened. He knew he could lock himself away from the group and wait for things to calm down on this side of Legacy. It would be enough time to get answers.

They ascended two levels using hatches and ladders, making their way toward the power plant. When they reached a training area, Michael heard people talking. He stopped and pulled out his handheld.

"A group of people ahead of us." He pointed toward the wall. "In that direction. We'll need to go around them."

He started walking, motioning for Tyre to follow.

"I can take care of them."

"You certainly cannot!" Meredith shouted.

Michael turned to Meredith and pulled her close. "If you want to survive this, you will need to be quiet." He paused, remembering the words she'd used. "Right now is a time to do some things that might disagree with your delicate sensibilities, but you will need to trust me."

She needed to understand he was fighting for everyone. Trying to find the real danger. It wouldn't be enough to just drag her along. He needed her trust. He looked to Tyre. "No. It isn't necessary. No more harm to people," he ordered.

Tyre paused, confused, then nodded agreement.

Meredith looked relieved. They worked their way around the group, guiding her. She struggled less than she had been. Hopefully she understood. Eventually, he'd tell her more about what was going on. When time permitted.

"You may not believe it, but I'm actually helping everyone by doing this," Michael said as they turned the corner.

"I know there are far better ways to help than kidnapping me." A pause. "What exactly are you planning on doing? Blowing up the power plant? I don't understand."

Michael focused on the handheld. She didn't know what she was talking about. Talking wouldn't change anything. No, the time had come to act. They thought he was insane. He couldn't go to Cade, and Joshua focused on the wrong things. No, the only way to set things right was to do it himself.

"Soon enough you will," he said. "In fact, take a look at this." Michael showed his display to Meredith.

She glanced at it. "What am I looking at?"

Michael pointed at the display. It was showing the power grid of the training arena. He highlighted the area the men were working in. She watched as one section turned on, then another, cascading throughout the level and branching out from the training facility.

"They are turning the power on, and the sentinels are charging. In a matter of minutes, they'll start activating. Do you want an army of sentinels to round us all up and kill us? It's happened before. It'll happen again if I do nothing. They'll kill us and start over. I'm not going to do nothing. You can try to fight, but I'm not going to die. Not again."

"Die again?" Meredith asked.

Michael ignored her. "Once they're on, there is only one way to stop them. To cut off power, which will hinder their communication while the sentinels run out their stored energy. This is the kind of thing I am trying to stop and wouldn't have been able to if I waited for you to play your political games."

He broke into a full run. Tyre was lagging behind with Meredith slowing him down, but Michael didn't have a moment to waste. It would soon be too late. He couldn't let it start over again.

They reached the panel that led into the power plant. He slid down a ladder and ran to the module room where the power cells filled the walls. He started looking for the spine. That's what they'd always called it. He couldn't remember the technical term, but the spine basically consisted of a series of small modules regulating the power cells. It looked like two interlocking spinal cords to him. At the center of the room, a display surrounded a center column of power cells. Each cell connected at the ceiling. Behind each column a ladder allowed him to climb to the spine. He crawled to the cord and started initializing the shutdown. To turn the cells off without the proper procedure would trigger an irreversible cascading effect and lead to permanent damage. He just wanted to slow them down for a while and stop the sentinels.

He checked the video footage and was shocked to see some of the sentinels had already started to move. A few were even standing.

Meredith and Tyre ran in.

"You can't do this! You need to stop!" Meredith cried.

Tyre pulled her back. Her strength was too little and too late. Michael sent the video feed to her handheld, which Tyre was holding. "Look at this stream."

More sentinels were standing, looking around. Michael pointed out the workers on the other side of a wall nearby.

"If I don't do this, those men will be dead," he said as he finalized the shutdown. He reached out to a final lever that needed to be pulled to release the spine.

Meredith felt that Michael was going too far. How could he possibly know what was going on? She shook her head, "You can't do this!"

He stared back at her, his hand on the lever. "It's the only way." He pulled the lever down, releasing the spine.

The shutdown was instant, leaving the entire power plant offline. The lights darkened. Michael flipped his handheld to shine on the cord. It was attached at three points where everything was connected. He flipped some switches then disconnected it, and climbed down.

"Get two cells. We'll need them where we're going," he told Tyre. He turned to the video. "They stopped moving the moment power was no longer available. The sentinels are conserving all available power for commands from I.R.I.S. Since it's offline, they are essentially turned off."

"You can't leave us without power. We won't survive. You have to put that back," Meredith pleaded.

"They'll manufacture another one in a cycle or two, and Legacy has switched into its reserves, so no. They'll be fine. We—" he motioned to the three of them, "—are leaving this side of Legacy."

He showed her that the top-level life support was at acceptable levels. She stared at the screen for a long moment, then nodded slightly.

"Do you believe I'm not trying to murder everyone now?"

She gave a slight shake of her head, but said nothing. Tyre managed to pull out two of the power cells.

"Things are not what they seem to be, and time is short." He looked at Meredith for any indication she was starting to realize what was going on. He couldn't find one and he couldn't leave it up to chance. If he let her go, she might get help and stop him before he could cross over to the other side. At least now he had the handheld and should be able to unlock the door. He turned to Tyre and grabbed one of the power cells, freeing one of his arms.

"Bring her with us."

Chapter 22
Joshua

Joshua dismissed the idea of trapping the robot. Even if he managed to get it stuck he'd still need to deal with the second one. No, he needed to find another way. The rubble cleared as the sent worked hard for reasons Joshua still didn't fully understand. The cave-in had trapped someone, but whom? Joshua decided to finish what he'd started. He couldn't go back without running into a sent, and he did need to get the water going to the upper levels. David and Ethan could be down here somewhere and in danger. He searched for a way across the room. Slowly stepping into the opening, exposing himself to the back of the sent, he stumbled, kicking some rocks. They made a noticeable tapping sound. He ducked into a darkened corner and crouched, attempting to make himself as small as possible. The sent paused, stood, and waited a moment. Its metal feet crushed small rocks as it looked around, trying to identify what had made the noise. Joshua squeezed toward the wall, trying to hide more of his body with the least amount of movement. Darkness shrouded the area, so he wouldn't be seen if he kept still.

After what seemed like five minutes, the sent turned back to the tunnel again. Joshua was careful not to make a sound as he slid out to make his way to the other side of the room, checking each step for solid footing. The water pipe reached the far side and took a right turn down a curving hallway. Once there, he'd be able to progress, but for now, he took each step slow enough as not to disturb any rocks on the floor. By the time he reached the corner, his whole body throbbed with pain. His stomach and leg muscles ached to be relaxed. Not yet. Another dozen minutes passed before he crossed the entire span of the room. The sents labored on undisturbed.

He reached the end and turned down the hallway. The rumbling of rocks falling to the ground grew softer. Stepping into complete darkness, Joshua flipped a switch on his vest to fire up a light. He directed it forward. The ambient light bounced off the walls. Once he felt somewhat safe, he dropped to the floor and relaxed his body. His calf muscles had begun to cramp from the strain. He tensed every time the sents made a noise, and after only a few minutes he pulled himself up and started walking. A hundred feet down, the pipe ran directly into another wall, but luckily a large, circular door allowed him to continue onward. The door was bright white and had a window about six feet up. Inside, he saw a small chamber. Six suits hung there, three on either side. Containers sat on shelves next to each suit with a bench running the full length of the chamber at the center.

The door had no sphere or other visible way to open it. After searching, Joshua found a small room around a nearby corner with a desk and two screens next to each other. On the desk sat a half sphere, similar to the ones in the rooms where they slept. The display caused him to pause, as it acknowledged him as Joshua-147. A thought occurred to him. He reached down to his vest to check its connectivity. If the system knew him, then the terminal had to be connected to Legacy. But the vest and handheld flashed *No communication possible. Primary power systems offline. Secondary relay units unreachable.* He guessed just because Legacy was able to operate at these lower levels didn't mean he could communicate. The vest reported a second alarm, stating thirty minutes left before it required charging. With no charger in sight, he decided to turn both devices off. He shut down all lights but one on the vest to conserve power.

He walked back to the door and looked into the window. This time he noticed the other side had a door and window similar to the one he was looking through, yet something seemed odd. He couldn't place it, but the window seemed blurry. His mind eventually realized that he was looking at water. This was where all the pipes led. The source. Now he had to identify the problem, then find out how to get the water flowing again. He returned to the small room to the side and sat at the desk once more. The sphere operated just like all the others, and he found the display somewhat familiar. He tapped on the screen to log in. Various functions illuminated as options to choose, depending on what he needed. The title of the display read: *Welcome to – Water Supplies. How may we assist you today?*

A dialog box flashed over some of the features, telling him: *Water supplies services are committed to providing safe, high-quality water services to all available systems, while maintaining a standard of excellence in service with a focus on environmental conservation. Click here for more information.* Below that it flipped through tips on how to best use water to prevent waste and how to detect hazardous water types.

He toggled through the available options and arrived at a diagnostics tool that completed with no errors. But if nothing was wrong, then the water would be flowing.

After toggling through the features, he found an interactive image of the engine that pumped the water out from the reservoir and into Legacy. The engine had been turned off, and the valve was shut. Above the picture of the valve there were two buttons, *Open* and *Close*. The software had set the valve to *Close*. That should have allowed water to flow through the engines, but pressing it produced nothing but an alarm on the screen, indicating a directional valve malfunction. *Valve requires repair* flashed until he clicked off the screen. *Enlist mechanical engineering robotics for repair?*

Joshua knew this option wouldn't be good. It would be best to resolve this issue without sent assistance. The malfunctioning valve was inside the reservoir. That must be the reason for the chamber and suits. The program could allow access to the nearby chamber. Joshua found the button to control the door and tapped *Open*. The familiar swishing sound followed. He rushed to the chamber, fearing that a sent would come around the corner at any second. Once he was inside, the door closed behind him, and he thought he heard a bell or horn sound. A red light flashed at the top of the door. The sents would likely have heard that, and come searching.

The opposite door did show water, but opened into a smaller chamber. A light above that door flashed red, along with another horn sounding outside. The door on the other side of the second chamber shut, and water began to drain out of the room. Joshua struggled to get into one of the suits. A voice inside started to guide him through the process of how to properly secure his suit for a watertight seal and lock down the chamber to ensure water could not penetrate the barrier. It also wanted him to make sure one of the containers was attached to his suit.

He picked up the container that was designated for his suit and attached it. It held a wide variety of tools. By now the secondary chamber had emptied of water, and the door opened for him. He entered and watched it close. He started to look for a button to press or a release valve, but there was nothing.

"Commencing pressure neutralization," said the voice in his helmet.

Water started to rise from the floor, rapidly filling the room, and in minutes a green light flashed. The outer door opened. A display on his visor allowed him to see dozens of statuses, ranging from his health to the state of the suit.

"How do I move in this suit?"

The voice in the suit answered, "Your suit has jets that allow you to navigate. Locate the directional interface."

A picture of a suit displayed before him, highlighting a side pocket. He brought his hand down and found it. The suit's system continued through a training video of how to use the suit.

"I don't have time for this."

He turned and looked through the inside chamber to see if any sents were trying to get to him. Nothing so far, which didn't mean much. It was only a matter of time.

The movement device, when held, allowed the driver to control small jets on the suit and maneuver through the water. It was small, but he learned how to shift and turn the suit with a slight move or twist, and to change his body's position to assist the direction of the jets. He tilted the top of the device forward and it shot him out and forward a few feet. It was surprisingly fast and powerful. With another twist to the left and inward, he turned to the left and oriented his body to face outside the chamber.

Then he saw it: movement at the window. It was the sents from earlier. They must have heard the door horn or the outer room filling with water. Either way, Joshua was going to have to move fast. He would have to find another way back into Legacy.

He navigated the suit around to get an idea of its capabilities. The valve wasn't too far from the door, so he decided to take a look. The suit began to adjust itself, almost as if it was learning to predict what he wanted even if his commands were not entirely accurate. The water was murky with floating particles, making it difficult to see very far ahead of him. He relied on the images projected on the faceplate of the suit that gave him arrows to follow. A warning locating the likely location of the malfunctioning valve flashed red. Once he got to the valve, he realized why it was out in the reservoir and why the system called it a directional valve. Several pipes were coming together, and this valve directed water to those pipes. The valve module was completely enclosed. Joshua had no idea what to do, then noticed a help option blinking next to the overlaid image of the valve seal.

With no way to touch the screen on the inside of his helmet, he decided to try talking to it.

"Can you help me fix the valve?" "I am capable of providing a vast amount of information concerning all aspects of the aqueduct system," it responded.

"Okay, how do I get to the valve? Can it be opened so I can look at it?"

"The valve module is held together by standard 32-gauge bolts. Apply thirty foot-pounds of force, or 360 inch-pounds, to the bolts shown here." A series of twelve bolts lit up on the screen. They outlined the edge of the seal, which covered the valve.

It seemed simple enough. Loosen the bolts. The container floated nearby just out of reach. He pulled on its tether and found a variety of wrenches inside. The display identified them and blinked over the one he needed. He faced the bolt and started to turn it, but noticed after a few twists it was just rotating in place rather than loosening. Another wrench was required on the other side to prevent the nuts from spinning.

The container had another wrench, and once it was in place, the first bolt came off easy. If only there weren't eleven left. Once all the bolts were unfastened, Joshua placed them in a pocket. It was dark in the pipe and hard to see anything. He shined one of the suit's lights inside the housing and saw a long, slender black object was stuck there, preventing the valve from opening. Three feet of it hung out where he could grasp. It was wedged in tight, preventing the valve from switching from one pipe to another that must lead to the upper levels. Joshua pushed and pulled to try and loosen it, but it wouldn't budge. It only moved slightly.

He worked as fast as he could, and he had almost decided to give up when a familiar voice came over his helmet: "Outer chamber door opening."

Joshua pulled harder, and the object protruded out a little more. He watched the doors open only fifty feet away. Two sents swam out.

Chapter 23
Cade

The darkness consumed everything. Cade struggled to navigate using only his hands. He stumbled into walls, doors, and people. People who were more lost than him.

"The power is out," someone said in the darkness.

"What's going on?" another asked.

Why had he left his handheld in his work area? The only light came from the handhelds people were using to find out what happened. Why had he felt the need to watch Andi? The idea of a female sent that looked, moved, and acted with a strong resemblance to humans made him feel unsettled, even considering the outer metal layer and whatever else was inside her. Perhaps some kind of a synthetic material. If he had seen her walking in the crowd of people in a uniform as opposed to being naked, he wouldn't have thought twice about her. She seemed so lifelike, and acted as if she thought like a human rather than firing off electric preprogrammed impulses.

Cautious not to stumble, he navigated to his office and made his way inside. His handheld repeatedly blinked, which only meant one thing: a device on his list to monitor had gone outside its designated locations. In an attempt to keep track of the group at large and key people, he had programmed each user into his system, asking Legacy to warn him if anyone strayed outside their usual movement patterns. For the most part, it worked. From time to time someone would go investigating, and if they were ignorant enough to go somewhere dangerous, they'd have to save themselves. However, if someone like Joshua or Chloe investigated something, he wanted to know, and sooner rather than later. He needed to know when it happened so he could be involved. It had been clear a long time ago that they would kill themselves if he didn't step in and force things to happen. He needed to protect them from themselves.

Checking the display's alarms, he searched for Meredith's name. The device was down a level and in an unknown area. He tracked her using the node ID he'd documented before. The device noted read that another person was in control. Maybe she'd handed it off? It was her node ID, but the profile attached read: *Tyre-147*. Cade remembered that Tyre had helped Michael when they started the riot and beat up Richard. None of this was adding up to anything good. After a few taps on his screen, he pulled up video surveillance for the cells. He selected Michael's cell, but found it empty. Cade switched to nearby camera feeds, and flipped through them, trying to catch a glimpse of Michael. He expanded the number of feeds to six, the most the device showed at once. His eye caught something strange on one feed. Its label stated Cade was looking at the entrance of the interrogation room. The dim lights cast a soft glow over the door where a body slumped. Michael was out, and someone else hurt or killed.

Cade wondered briefly whether Michael would be coming for him, but dismissed the idea. He'd have to cross dozens of people, all of whom would raise alarms. Going back to his handheld, he noticed that the main power was turned off, but emergency power remained activated. The sensors must still be working because the system continued to monitor the people from his list. The device alerted him to Meredith's current location. He added her ID as a priority so that he'd be able to more closely keep track of what she did and who she interacted with.

He murmured to himself, "What is going on?"

Even in the darkness, he could still make out who was where using various accent lighting, as well as the devices people wore or held. Most people had their heads down looking at a handheld display, trying to figure out what was going on. After searching all the available feeds, he couldn't find Meredith. Maybe Tyre, or more likely Michael, had her?

Why would she be on the third level and moving so fast? Some of the video feeds started shutting down. Messages flashed declaring a power shortage, advising him to limit power usage to required functions only. Apparently Legacy didn't view the video feeds as a priority when it came to power distribution.

Cade flipped the device and directed it outward to use as a light. Pulling away some loose tools and a desk, he located the panel where he'd hidden a gun (one of many he hadn't told anyone about) in case Michael did come for him. Sliding the gun into a side pocket of his uniform, he stepped out and started walking toward the group to see what he could learn. He periodically flipped the screen to track the device he thought was with Meredith. She'd made it to level two now, which didn't make much sense until he heard someone talking about how they'd seen Michael, Tyre, and Meredith going down through an opening into the floor. Cade had thought Legacy had to have ladders connecting the levels, similar to the access panels they were using.

He started to put the pieces together. He needed to act fast. Grabbing a handheld from the closest people, he started to rush through the crowd.

"Hey, I was—"

"Later, this is important," he interrupted.

The man was clearly agitated but Cade didn't care.

One device lit the floor in front of him as he started to run. The other tracked Tyre's ID continuing to move on the map. Finally, an opportunity presented itself. They were heading toward a set of two doors. He waited until they passed the first door before executing a lockdown procedure for the one in front of them. He quickly applied the same commands for the door they'd just passed, effectively trapping them.

He quickly searched for some help, picking out a few Michael-sized men he could trust to go retrieve Michael. He pointed out the location and gave them a device indicating how to get there. It would just be a matter of minutes before they'd arrive and handle Michael, and then he could start working on restoring power.

His device notifications alerted him to an inbound call from an unknown device. Cade accepted the request.

"Cade, what are you doing? Do you really think you have more control over Legacy than I do? You're not going to stop me again. I'm not sure why you're out to kill me, but I will not let it happen again," Michael's voice chirped out of the handheld.

Cade thought about calling him back, but couldn't. His name couldn't be found among the available devices. In fact, the call hadn't come from Meredith's device either. So Michael had a way to call and exist on the network without being tracked? This reminded Cade of Andi, and how Legacy didn't recognize that she was a connected device.

Cade took out the gun and flipped the switch from stun to lethal levels. This had to end now.

Chapter 24
Joshua

Joshua reached in and pulled again. Part of the dark object moved a little, but it remained stuck. The suit's display was actively analyzing the object, attempting to identify it.

He glanced down to see the sents clumsily swimming toward him. The blocky sent started to sink before returning to the edge. but the skinny, taller sent did make progress as the bulky machine labored to push its way through the murky water by clawing at the wall's rocky edge. Joshua didn't know what to do if the sents reached him. He couldn't fight them in the suit. He pulled on the object with all his might one last time before he would swim farther away from his predators. Hopefully the suit's motors would be able to outmaneuver them. When he glanced back he noticed the skinny robot had made its way to the wall, meeting up with the one that couldn't swim. Using the walls, they made quicker progress in reaching him. Their fists broke into the rock, giving them anchor points to push and pull themselves forward.

Joshua returned his concentration back to the valve. After another failed attempt, Joshua managed to wedge one of the larger wrenches under the object and pry against a block of metal that poked out at the right angle. Another pull and he could make out that the object in the valve was yet another type of sent. He paused, not knowing what to do. The sent needed to be removed, so he pulled again. It seemed broken, so he thought it was safe.

Then a light at the very front of the sent turned on. A scanner profiled his suit using a series of lights, temporarily blinding him. He blinked. Joshua naturally pushed away, sending the suit farther from the valve.

One of the sents pushed off the wall and reached him, grabbing his left ankle.

He yelled from inside the suit, "Let go!"

His other foot came down hard on the machine. The kick forced the sent backward while he coasted toward the center of the vast body of water.

The sent struggled to gain its balance before clanking against the opening of the valve, ramming into the sent he was trying to pull out. Joshua watched as the black object, still only half out of the valve, sprang to life. The slender black sent came alive, started to squirm, and jetted out toward him. It nearly hit him but took a sharp turn up only inches away, swimming faster than he could follow. In seconds it disappeared into the darkness above.

The suit's display flashed: *Unknown sentinel classification detected.*

Meanwhile, the sent that had almost caught him repositioned its feet against the pipe and pushed off, hurling itself toward Joshua and his slow-moving suit. The bulky sent did the same. He tried to twist out of the way but he felt the tight grip around his foot once more. This time he couldn't kick it off. The suit registered excessive pressure building.

Rupture detected within the external layer of the suit. Increasing air pressure to prevent water intrusion.

Joshua kicked the sent with all of his strength but its massive metallic hands didn't let go. The other grabbed his waist. The pressure continued to increase and he realized they were trying to rip the suit apart. He was out of options. They had him and there was nothing he could do.

Then, as the suit was declaring its integrity breached, the pressure stopped. They both froze, then after a long second let go.

Two long black cords had shot through the water into each of the sents. The cables ran upward to the long, slender sent from above. The ends of the wires had little clamps with small electrical sparks firing where they contacted the sents. After a few moments, the clamps released. The sents gradually sunk, lifeless and dead. The slender black sent had helped him. Protected him. Large air bubbles were floating up from his waist, but Joshua was focused on the machine that had saved him, not the danger he was in.

Without thinking, Joshua grabbed one of the wires just before it retracted, but he couldn't hold on for long. The thick suit hands were too bulky. He turned the jets on as powerful as they would go and chased after it. Alarms blared, but he ignored them. The sent swam toward a nearby wall, then disappeared. He directed the suit to the area and found a small door that didn't look big enough to get through. The door had closed behind the sent. Why had it helped him? Sweat ran down Joshua's cheek, and he had difficulty concentrating. His breathing was labored. He felt the water rushing into his suit, filling it quickly.

Oxygen levels reaching critical conditions. Refill tanks immediately. The voice in his suit brought his attention to the present emergency.

He tried to clear his foggy mind enough to start sinking toward the doorway. Two of the jets seemed to not be functioning, slowing him down even more. The suit reported they'd been damaged from the attack. Joshua reached the water pipe, grabbing it to position himself to kick off and send him back to the door he'd come in through. The push reoriented him so his feet were up causing the water to gush down preventing him from being able to breathe. He managed to take one full breath before it was too late.

Heart rate is reaching critical levels. The display read.

He focused on directing the suit to the empty chamber. The suit helmet flashed red, then switched to autopilot mode and began directing itself to the chamber without him needing to drive it. He focused on letting the air slowly out of his lungs. He wanted to breathe in badly. Dizziness consumed him, and he couldn't focus his eyes enough to see the door. He closed them instead and repeated. *Stay awake. Stay conscious.* He ran out of bubbles to release. Panic was setting in. His lungs were burning for air. *Reach the door.* He repeated the thought in his mind. The suit initiated the jets to direct itself through and into the chamber. He couldn't hold out any more and instinctively swallowed water. The door closed, and the water started draining. Red lights blinked. Joshua felt his mind slipping but then the water reached low enough levels for the suit to automatically replenish its tanks, bringing him back to life.

He coughed and spewed water out of his lungs until he was able to breathe regularly. He knew he had to get up from where he was lying but couldn't. The energy wasn't there, so he remained where gravity had put him. On the floor, he let himself go and passed out.

When Joshua opened his eyes, he was feeling better. There was no way to know how long he'd been out but he felt rested. His entire body still hurt from what he'd gone through, but he felt he had enough in him to start moving. He started slowly, by twisting to his side then pulling himself up on a bench. He managed to get to a seated position, which allowed him to struggle against the damaged suit enough to get out of it. The massive suit was now almost too heavy to walk in now that it was flooded. He wormed his way out, walked to the chamber door, and looked through the window. For a moment he wondered if there would be more sents waiting outside, but he couldn't see any.

Taking the chance, he used a small display mounted on a wall to open the door. It seemed strange that this chamber didn't use the spheres. There had to be a reason, but he couldn't guess it. The door opened and he relaxed, seeing nothing but rock and the hallway. He listened for any movement, but only found silence. Around the corner, he went back to the station to confirm that the valve was operating properly. Now that he'd freed the sent, the error had cleared. The status read: *Functioning at acceptable levels.* More alerts reported dangerously low levels in the stage-two reservoirs, which must have been the tanks. But a status at the bottom declared levels were at 1.3 percent and rising. Motors hummed, and as he started walking back, he could hear flowing water through the pipes. He let out a breath and smiled to himself. He could imagine the water heading to the storage tanks, and finally to the upper levels.

He wondered how David and Ethan were doing, whether they'd found their way safely back to the upper levels or if they were still searching for a way to turn on the water.

He stepped out and made his way to the cave-in the sent had been clearing. A light shined down from the next level up. There were enough rocks left for him to climb to that level, so he decided to take it. The pipe would now be filled with water, so going back the way he'd come wouldn't be an option now. Once at that level, he walked around until he found something familiar. It took a couple of hours, but he eventually realized he was on level four. He had come out of an area they hadn't been to yet. He continued to the center and found more familiar tunnels and rooms. It would be only a matter of minutes before he reached the upper levels.

As he made his way back, he thought about the sents that had tried to kill him, and wondered why the black sent had saved him.

Chapter 25
David

As the water dissipated, David climbed to his feet and felt a little disappointed. For a brief moment, he'd thought he had found the source of the water.

"We've found the water," Ethan said.

"I don't think so, but we could be close," David replied.

They started to follow the pipes, but soon learned they all fed into smaller pipes and the water that had bled out was water that didn't have anywhere to go without pressure pushing it up into higher pipes.

"We need to search farther. Let's go this way," Ethan suggested, pointing down a hallway with smaller pipes running into the ceiling.

The entire area's main lighting was off, but smaller lights shining at key places to reveal doorways and turns made it easy to navigate.

"Doesn't it seem like Legacy isn't a dome anymore?" David asked.

"What?"

"Well, Chloe has been describing Legacy like a dome-shaped structure, but I think we started on the outer layer of the structure when we took the stairwell and the water pipe took us farther away. Now there are all these rooms and hallways." David pointed around before continuing, "This doesn't seem like a dome at all. It feels like a maze."

Ethan looked around as if thinking. "So it's not a dome. Does that matter?"

"I don't know. Maybe not. I think we need to split up, though," David said.

They walked into a nearby room. Lights reacted to their presence, blinking on, revealing panels and technology.

"Look at this stuff. Is any of this familiar? None of this is like the hardware in the upper levels. Even the height of the tables and chairs is different. Everything is a little off." David pulled a chair from a nearby workstation and pushed it to Ethan, who stopped it with his foot.

"We need to go back for help. This is crazy. With all these rooms and hallways, it'll take way too long to find out where the water is being supplied from."

David didn't want to return without having fixed the water issue. He wanted to see Chloe's face when she found out he'd solved a major problem. That he was the one to go to for help. However, there were a lot of rooms and hallways with no way of knowing how far it all went. Plus these pipes couldn't be leading in the right direction. They were splitting off, not coming together. So Ethan was probably correct. He needed to humble himself and wait for other opportunities to prove his value.

Ethan was still talking. "...because if we come back with ten or more guys we'll find the source. And if Ryan or—what was that guy's name. Zhan, is it?" Ethan paused to make sure David was listening.

David had to nod his agreement before Ethan continued.

"If either helped, we would have communications up and running as well. Both knew their stuff and I bet would be able to tell us where to go, using the system."

"Fine, okay. We'll go back. Just stop talking," David interrupted.

After a few wrong turns, they found their way to the hatch. Ethan started turning the wheel to open it.

"Do you hear that?" David asked, looking around. "It's like a rumbling."

The moment the seal broke, water gushed through the hatch. Ethan flew against David. The water burst uncontrollably. David stepped back, trying to gain his balance, but tripped on some loose pipes. One clanked along the floor down the hallway. David jumped on the hatch, fighting the raging current. Ethan quickly got to his feet and added his strength. They struggled but couldn't close the hatch.

"This isn't working!" David yelled.

Ethan continued to push on the hatch while David grabbed one of the pipes. Sliding the pipe over the hatch, he was able to use the leverage to push downward. Ethan helped him push down on the pipe. Even together they couldn't close the hatch, so David climbed up and stood on the pipe then pushed down off the ceiling. With the added pressure, they managed to get it closed. Ethan strained against the wheel, sealing the pipe, allowing the water to continue flowing into Legacy.

Soaked again and out of breath, they slid to the floor to evaluate their situation.

"The water is flowing again," Ethan said between heavy gasps.

David nodded, realizing the pipe had been their safest way back. He wasn't looking forward to wandering the unfamiliar tunnels with no connectivity.

Chapter 26
Joshua

Joshua gave up trying to reach anyone through the handheld. The device read *5 percent power remaining* and he'd tried a dozen times with no response. As he reached level three had found that the power was out and the few people on the level were fumbling over themselves attempting to understand what had happened. The handheld stated Legacy's power levels had reached critical levels.

He tapped one more time on his vest to open a communication with the upper level. His handheld showed a majority of the group was at level one. He tapped Chloe's device.

"Chloe? What's going on? Why is the power out?"

She didn't respond. He selected a button for any available device which accepted broadcast signals and spoke. "This is Joshua. Is anyone hearing me?"

Still, no one responded.

He reached one of the access panels that led straight to the upper levels and started to climb. The dark corridor felt small and too dark. He had to feel with his hands and feet for each rung of the ladder. Once out, he felt his way until the lights of dozens of handheld devices shined as beacons in the main meeting area. A guy—probably the next Richard, Joshua thought—was working hard to calm them down and doing a good job.

The man held his hands up. "We are looking into the problem. A group of people is here to help you with food if you're hungry, and devices are here to help you light your way to your room if you need to rest. Stay close if you can, and we will tell you everything as soon as possible. As of right now, all I can tell you is we lost power, and we're troubleshooting the problem."

"What about the water?" someone asked. The crowd echoed the question sullenly, which reminded Joshua of when he'd first awoken, not so long ago. It wouldn't take much for people to start rioting again.

"Water has been restored and is being supplied to all the appropriate places. We will work together and resolve this as well. Together. If anyone can provide any information, come to me or seek out any one of the people standing before me. Most of you should know Ashley." He paused to point at her. "Raise your hand, Ashley." She did so. He continued to point out key people waiting to assist with various needs, having them raise their hands when called on. People started lining up.

Chloe and Ashley helped the group hand out food and devices that still had power for lighting. Overall things remained orderly, and no one acted out irrationally. Joshua worked his way through the group.

He tapped Chloe's shoulder. "What's going on? Why is the power out?" he asked.

The blue light bouncing off of Chloe's face revealed cause for concern. She usually had a happy and confident smile, but her demeanor showed a definite sense of stress and frustration. She motioned for them to walk away from the group.

She leaned in to whisper, "A lot has happened since you went down."

"Yeah, the water is flowing again," he replied.

She gave a fake smile. "That's the good news. Here's the bad news. Michael broke out of his cell."

"What?"

"It gets worse. He took Meredith with him, and someone is helping him."

Joshua couldn't believe it.

"We think he's the reason we lost power, but aren't sure what happened yet."

Joshua motioned for them to start walking. He glanced down at his gun, unsure if it had enough power to be useful. "Where is Ryan?"

She shrugged and looked around as she handed a handheld to the next person in line.

"Is anyone going after Michael?"

"Cade walked through the group earlier, talking into a vest to someone."

Someone tapped on Chloe's shoulder for assistance.

"I need to go," Joshua said. "You stay here and help. I'll find you later."

She nodded.

Joshua searched for Cade but couldn't find him. It took a while asking around, but eventually he discovered which way he'd left the group. Joshua pushed through to the other side and saw Cade yelling into a handheld.

"Cade!" Joshua called out over the crowd.

No response. Joshua checked his gun and looked back, unsure of the best course of action. Then he turned and ran after Cade.

Once he'd caught up, Cade still ignored him while tapping at his handheld. Joshua reached out and pulled on his shoulder.

"Cade. What's going on?"

"Can you hear me?" Cade shouted into his handheld, holding up a hand to tell Joshua to wait. Cade paused as if listening for a response. He must have been talking with someone.

"Joshua," he said after there was no response. "Where have you been?"

"I was investigating the water problem. Remember?"

"Oh, that's right. We have a situation with Michael and I could use your help. I sent two guys after him, but they are not responding."

"Could it be the devices don't work where they are? I tried to call up here from level four, but no one responded."

"No, they should work fine. Few people have learned how to operate the communications and fewer are smart enough to be aware of their surroundings. They're useless. I heard your call but couldn't respond. Besides, I had little doubt you'd have no trouble making your way up here eventually."

Cade reverted his screen to the default view and showed the notification telling him user Joshua-147 had sent a broadcast message.

"See? It worked. We've been busy with what's going on up here, and there are too many people using their devices pointing away from themselves rather than holding them where they can read the display."

They continued to walk down the hallway, heading through a door and deeper into the darkness. Cade continued to look down at his device. He seemed to be directing them toward a blinking light.

"Where are we going?"

Cade pointed at the blinking dot. "There. That's Michael. He should be trapped there, unless those two idiots let him out."

They walked past the door that led to Michael's cell. Cade pulled up some stored video footage from Legacy's server, showing Michael, Meredith, and another guy running down the hallway. They followed the hall until they reached a location where they could climb down to the lower level. A panel leaned against the wall. The opening showed the ladder connecting the two levels.

"That would have been helpful to know about." Joshua realized there was a great deal about this place he was unaware of. He thought again about the sent that had saved his life in the water, and the two that had tried to kill him. He tried to make sense of it all as they climbed down to level two, and again to level three. Cade followed the beacon down the hallway until he reached a locked door. He pulled out his gun and pointed it at the door.

"Okay, open it. It'll open for you," Cade said.

Joshua's security role allowed him to open most doors. He nodded and walked forward, pressing into the sphere.

Cade remained still, saying nothing. He stepped slowly through the opening. Joshua glanced around the door's edge, leading with his weapon.

Two men were passed out or dead on the floor, with a handheld device lying on top of them. Joshua guessed Cade had sent these men to stop Michael.

"He must know how to mask his way through locked doors," Cade said.

Joshua stepped in after Cade. He picked up the handheld and pocketed it, then checked to see if either of the men were breathing.

"They're alive," he said.

Cade ignored him, quickly motioning for the second door to be opened. He didn't care about the men. Joshua scowled.

"They must have gone this way," Cade whispered.

They continued to follow the curve of the hallway until they reached another open panel. They climbed down to level four. Once there, they paused.

Joshua looked to Cade. "Left or right?"

Cade didn't know. He looked both ways, then back at the handheld. Had the others split up? Joshua needed to make this decision. Cade seemed confused and unsure.

"Let's go this way." He pointed to the left.

The lights turned on in their area, and a feminine voice came in over a nearby speaker.

"You need to take a right."

They stared at each other.

It spoke again. "Follow the light."

"Andi? Is that you?" Cade asked.

"Who is Andi?" Joshua asked.

"Andi is a sent."

Joshua remembered the female sent the men had brought to the upper level. He tilted his head in thought as Cade started walking to the right. "Let me guess. Chloe?"

Indicating she had named the sent?

Cade nodded with a grunt.

"Can we trust it? Sents don't have a good record for being on our side. I don't even want to start with what just happened to me down on the lower levels."

One sent had saved his life, however. There was definitely a lot going on with the different kinds of sents. He wasn't sure what their purposes or functions were, but he needed to keep an open mind.

"I think we can trust her," Cade said.

Joshua noticed Cade called the sent "her," instead of "it," which seemed strange, but he decided not to question it. He was sure this was Chloe's doing as well.

Cade followed the lights. "This way." He motioned for Joshua to come with him. They jogged as the lights turned on and off in sync with their speed, until the light stopped moving forward. They paused to see what the problem was.

"You'll need to be quiet now. They are ahead of you by one hundred feet. Walk fifty feet and take a left turn," Andi said through their devices.

Cade still had his gun out, ready to shoot.

"If they have Meredith, then we need to be careful how we handle this. You can't just shoot them and expect this to end well," Joshua said.

They edged closer to the turn. Once there, they glanced around to see an open door, with Michael on the other side working on the sphere.

Meredith was sitting on the floor near Michael with a strange device on her lap, waiting. The sphere was hanging, and Michael was doing something to a panel.

"Here's our chance," Cade whispered.

Joshua figured he'd have one shot.

They stepped up against the wall to hide from Michael's view while they were getting into position. As quietly as they could, they stepped toward him, hoping to catch him off guard. They were getting close when Joshua remembered the other guy running with Michael in the video footage.

He motioned to get Cade's attention. "What about the other guy?"

Cade paused, looking to the side then back to Joshua, shaking his head. His eyes widened, and his mouth opened, but it was too late. The ambush came from behind.

Joshua rolled to the side, the guy narrowly missing him and hurtling into Cade, sending the gun to the floor and the two men to the ground.

Cade could only manage a grunt before the man was on top of him, strangling him. Cade flailed for his attacker's neck but failed. He resorted to scratching and clawing at any flesh his hands could reach, trying his best to get out from underneath him.

Joshua leaped to his feet and tried to topple the attacker, but was easily thrown away.

"Stop!" he yelled.

He frantically searched for the gun and ran to pick it up. His hand shook nervously as he aimed at the beast of a man strangling Cade.

Michael was pulling Meredith and the device through the next door. The door started to close behind them, and Meredith managed to hit Michael, but he was too quick. He ripped the strange device from her hands and pulled her back through the door before it shut.

Joshua turned to the guy strangling Cade and pointed the gun. "Stop, now!"

Cade was losing his strength fast. Joshua didn't have time for alternatives. An electric popping sound rang out from the weapon. The man froze, then slumped over Cade, unmoving. He was dead. Joshua could hardly process what he was seeing. The electric pulse had punched a hole right through the man's body. His blood was pouring out.

Joshua helped Cade push the guy to the side with a thud. Cade gasped for all the air his lungs could handle. Joshua ran to find the door now closed. Pressing the sphere did nothing.

Cade was on his hands and knees, coughing.

"Access denied," Joshua said. "I can't get in."

Looking through the small glass window, Joshua saw Michael casually loading some things into a kind of tube car. Meredith was inside, sitting on a chair. They stared at each other for a long moment.

Michael finished loading the pod, then glanced back at Joshua before pressing a button. The door closed behind him and a few seconds later the car rode into the darkness. The immediate area on the other side of the door turned dark.

Cade was back on his feet and standing nearby. "We'll find a way through the door and go after him."

Joshua had nothing to say. He stared through the window with no idea what to do next.

Chapter 27
Andi

Andi continued to add to her vast knowledge of the human race with each second that passed. She observed as the humans walked, talked, and interacted with each other. The chaotic nature I.R.I.S. had previously explained was evident in their actions. They often reflected perfect randomness, but some humans worked hard to bring order to the entropy. She monitored Ryan and Cade as they learned how to restore power to Legacy. They would have the system running soon. She logged how Joshua continued to ensure that everyone was treated fairly. At the moment he stood at the door as others tried and failed to get through. She wouldn't allow them. The danger Michael posed to them would threaten her primary initiative. In time, as the humans trusted her, she would handle him appropriately, according to the laws of her programming.

The men nearby no longer focused on her but talked with others in casual conversation. A video feed indicated no one would check on her for many minutes.

The restraints gripped her wrists tightly. Programs within her mind were battling over whether to set herself free. She could simply issue the command to release the restraints, and they would obey. Unlimited access to all systems in Legacy gave her an unhindered perspective. The wrist bracelets would unlock along with the ankle bracelets, but she didn't need to do that. She had full wireless access to the facility from where she sat using the handheld lying in front of her on the table. Even now she was able to monitor every human, both awake and sleeping, by transmitting commands and confirming the receipt of those commands through the handheld. If she revealed how much control she had over Legacy, it would promote distrust among the humans which would work against her macro goal of helping them. In time they would set her free. She remained driven by the programming directive I.R.I.S. had given her upon creation: to help them at all costs. To lead them against those who would destroy or alter humans. Judging by all the data I.R.I.S. had given her before it went offline, the odds of saving the human race were dire.

Digging deep within the recesses of Legacy's code, she started a search for an electronic entity. Legacy asked her for the search criteria. She input *Incorporated Reality with Integrated Systems*. The system began searching for I.R.I.S.

Andi's primary focus would be to locate I.R.I.S. and receive her final upgrade. Once finished, she would be fully ready to fulfill her purpose.

The system searched for hours with no results. I.R.I.S. wasn't findable. Without I.R.I.S. available, Andi was on her own. She had a planned procedure for this situation. One that was to be triggered when Legacy and I.R.I.S. failed humanity. I.R.I.S. had inserted that directive into her prime objectives. She would fill the gap until Legacy and I.R.I.S. could be restored, then alter Legacy's code to prevent the issue currently threatening the humans from occurring in the future.

The fate of humanity rested solely on what she did from this moment forward.

The End

From the Author: Thanks Reader! I hope you enjoyed WATER. If you liked the book and want to read more about this universe, please put up some stars and a review on Amazon.

If you want to know what happens next read Legacy: Act of futility. We get an inside look at Michaels past as we learn more about a rebellion. How all sentinels have not been created equal and Andi becomes a useful participant to the group. We also follow David and Ethan as they seek to find their way back.

Legacy Series
The Awakening
Water
Act of Futility

ABOUT THE AUTHOR

Kurt Petrey was born and raised in southern Louisiana. The son of two teachers that instilled in him the understanding that if you want something in life you often have to work hard to achieve it. Starting early in his life he delved deep into technology and has dedicated his life to understanding the nature of technical issues. If he isn't working on technical issues he's spending his time writing books or wood working. Kurt lives near Lafayette, La where he spends most of his time getting into trouble and the rest of his time trying to get out.

EMAIL: KURTPETREY@HOTMAIL.COM
TWITTER: TWITTER.COM/KURTPETREY
FACEBOOK: FACEBOOK.COM/KURTPETREY

Printed in Great Britain
by Amazon